She was about to meet the odious
Dr. Greg Hamilton.

Jane's eyes widened, and her heart skittered. He was too handsome for words!

"Hello."

He smiled, and Jane knew without a doubt from whom her baby niece had inherited her dimples. And his eyes were as green as little Joy's, too.

He reached for her hand and she automatically clasped his. His palm was warm against hers. Secure. Trustworthy. Her insides went utterly haywire.

"Jane," she said, relieved that she remembered her name. "Jane Dale." Her voice sounded whispery, halting.

"Nice to meet you." He paused. "Give me a moment to look at your file and then you can tell me what I can do for you today."

She was happy to give him as long as he needed. She needed some time herself. Time to bridle these unexpected and totally confusing emotions that were wreaking havoc on her nervous system....

SINGLE
DOCTOR
DADS

Next month, look for
The Doctor's Medicine Woman

Dear Reader,

As Silhouette's yearlong anniversary celebration continues, Romance again delivers six unique stories about the poignant journey from courtship to commitment.

Teresa Southwick invites you back to STORKVILLE, USA, where a wealthy playboy has the gossips stumped with his latest transaction: *The Acquired Bride*...and her triplet kids! *New York Times* bestselling author Kasey Michaels contributes the second title in THE CHANDLERS REQUEST... miniseries, *Jessie's Expecting*. Judy Christenberry spins off her popular THE CIRCLE K SISTERS with a story involving a blizzard, a roadside motel with one bed left, a gorgeous, honor-bound rancher...and his *Snowbound Sweetheart*.

New from Donna Clayton is SINGLE DOCTOR DADS! In the premiere story of this wonderful series, a first-time father strikes *The Nanny Proposal* with a woman whose timely hiring quickly proves less serendipitous and more carefully, *lovingly*, staged.... Lilian Darcy pens yet another edgy, uplifting story with *Raising Baby Jane*. And debut author Jackie Braun delivers pure romantic fantasy as a down-on-her-luck waitress receives an intriguing order from the man of her dreams: *One Fiancée To Go, Please*.

Next month, look for the exciting finales of STORKVILLE, USA and THE CHANDLERS REQUEST... And the wait is over as Carolyn Zane's BRUBAKER BRIDES make their grand reappearance!

Happy Reading!

Mary-Theresa Hussey

Mary-Theresa Hussey
Senior Editor

Please address questions and book requests to:
Silhouette Reader Service
U.S.: 3010 Walden Ave., P.O. Box 1325, Buffalo, NY 14269
Canadian: P.O. Box 609, Fort Erie, Ont. L2A 5X3

The Nanny Proposal

DONNA CLAYTON

SILHOUETTE *Romance*

Published by Silhouette Books

America's Publisher of Contemporary Romance

This book is dedicated to Peggy Moore
who is always ready and willing to straighten out
my twisted medical facts. Many thanks!

 SILHOUETTE BOOKS

ISBN 0-373-19477-3

THE NANNY PROPOSAL

Visit Silhouette at www.eHarlequin.com

Printed in U.S.A.

Books by Donna Clayton

DONNA CLAYTON

is proud to be a recipient of the Holt Medallion, an award honoring outstanding literary talent, for her Silhouette Romance *Wife for a While*. And seeing her work appear on the Waldenbooks Series Bestsellers List has given her a great deal of joy and satisfaction.

Reading is one of Donna's favorite ways to wile away a rainy afternoon. She loves to hike, too. Another hobby added to her list of fun things to do is traveling. She fell in love with Europe during her first trip abroad and plans to return often. Oh, and Donna still collects cookbooks, but as her writing career grows, she finds herself using them less and less.

Donna loves to hear from her readers. Please write to her care of Silhouette Books, 300 East 42nd Street, New York, NY 10017.

Greg Hamilton, M.D.
Family Practice
Philadelphia, Pennsylvania

Patient File

Name: <u>Me</u>

Diagnosis: <u>Super-stressed daddy of a ten-month-old toddler</u>

Symptoms: <u>Constantly late for work, bruises from tripping over</u>
<u>piles of baby laundry and toys, grumpy from</u>
<u>lack of sleep, just plain tired</u>

Prescription: <u>HIRE A NANNY. NOW!</u>

Dr. Greg Hamilton
Physician's Signature

Prologue

Greg Hamilton patted a healthy splash of aftershave on his smooth jaw as he stared into the mirror. Habit had him brushing his damp palms over his bare chest, then he picked up a comb and ran it through his wet hair.

He felt good. Like a man who had put in an intense week at work and was ready for a little fun on a Friday night.

His patients had kept him on his toes this week. He'd treated Mrs. Brown, with her just-give-me-a-pill attitude. The elderly woman he had just diagnosed as borderline diabetic refused to believe that her diet played an important role in her continuing a healthy life. He'd spent a great deal of time explaining the condition to her. But it seemed none of his arguments could curb the woman's taste for sweets.

And little Bobby Lee, whose bed-jumping escapade had earned him a fall that needed three stitches. Greg grimaced into the mirror, wondering why these kinds of things always happened right around eleven o'clock at night.

There had also been a myriad of coughs, colds, upper-respiratory infections and bouts of flu he'd treated. However, none of his patients concerned him more than young Tracy Morgan. The teen had an eating disorder. He was sure of it. But he'd had a devil of a time convincing her parents that their daughter had a problem at all. He'd begun explaining his diagnosis calmly, but their refusal to open their eyes and minds to the potentially deadly prognosis had frustrated him. He'd ended up frightening them into really listening to what he'd had to say. He'd felt badly when he'd seen the fear in their eyes, knowing he'd put it there. Parents never wanted to believe their child was in danger. But Greg had only acted out of concern for young Tracy. In the end, Mr. and Mrs. Morgan had agreed to take Tracy to see a specialist that Greg had recommended.

He sighed, tugging a fresh T-shirt over his head. Enough about his patients, he thought. He'd worked hard. Now it was time to relax and enjoy himself. And he had a date with a raven-haired beauty who was going to help him do just that.

As he fastened the buttons of his crisp white dress shirt, Greg once again thought about his medical practice—a practice he shared with his two best buddies in the whole world. He thought about his great apartment, positioned in the best possible location in the city. The hot little sports car he'd purchased just a few months ago.

Ah, yes, Greg sure did have the world by the tail.

And the very best part of being a successful bachelor doctor? Why, that would have to be the seemingly endless number of lovely ladies willing to spend Friday and Saturday evenings with him. A little dinner, a little dancing, a little kissing in the moonlight. He loved being a single guy.

It wasn't that he used or abused women. No way. In fact, he had a rule: no sex on the first—or second—date. The morning after the one and only time he'd broken the rule, he'd felt like a bum. A real heel. And on principle, he'd ended up reaffirming his faith in the "no sex without meaning" law. He simply enjoyed the company of females. Luckily, in this very enlightened age, there were plenty of women who felt free to enjoy the company of a man.

He buckled the belt around his waist, smoothed his palm over his taut abdomen, hand-pressing the pleats of his dress trousers, and then he slipped his feet into black Italian loafers. After one last glance at his reflection, he grabbed his suit jacket off the hanger, reached for his wallet and keys—and was stopped dead in his tracks by the doorbell.

Greg glanced at his watch, wondering who could be at his door as he shrugged on his jacket. Travis and Sloan, his friends and partners, knew he had a hot date tonight. Absently brushing his hand over one lapel, he moved down the hall and into the living room.

He heard the baby's cries before he even grasped the door handle. The child's wails had his brow furrowing. None of his neighbors had kids. A patient, maybe? But why hadn't his answering service notified him there was an emergency? Why wouldn't the baby's parents go directly to the hospital ER? Why would they show up here—

As the questions churned in his mind like the swirl caused when a boat oar is forced through river water, he gave the handle a quick twist and pulled open the door.

The woman was clearly annoyed. And vaguely familiar to him. Irritation pulsed from her in palpable waves. The baby girl in her arms was so upset her sobs were actually being released in tiny hiccups.

The professional medical practitioner in Greg immediately took over. Instinctively reaching for the child, he asked, "Is she ill?"

"No," the child's mother answered as she handed over the baby. "She's yours."

Greg's mouth dropped open as the baby squirmed in his arms. Shock paralyzed his vocal cords. Where did he know this woman from? he wondered. He racked his brain, trying to recall her name from the depths of his memory. And what on earth did she mean by what she'd said?

The woman then dropped a small suitcase at the threshold of the door and let the overstuffed diaper bag that hung on her shoulder slide to the floor beside it. Relieved of what seemed an overwhelming weight, she smiled for the first time, a gleam shining in her gaze—a gleam Greg could only describe as…triumphant. He got the distinct feeling she'd succeeded in some goal. Met some terribly stubborn and hundred-pound-weight-off-the-shoulder objective.

"Your daughter's name is Joy," the woman continued, "and I've decided it's high time for you to take her off my hands."

Chapter One

Greg burst through the glass double doors of the clinic. He didn't have to look at his watch to know he was late. His first patient would be waiting. His whole day's schedule shot. Again.

"Your first patient is waiting."

Rachel Richards, the office manager for the clinic, teased him with a disapproving click of her tongue.

"I know," he said in a rush. "I know."

"She's only a baby, Dr. Greg." Rachel reached out and took his daughter from him, grinning at the happy ten-month-old. "The way you're reacting, it's the end of the world."

A spontaneous gust of ironic laughter erupted from him. "Joy's arrival *was* the end of the world as I knew it." He softly added, "I'm trying to get used to this new planet called parenthood. Please have patience with me."

He felt as if he was whispering the plea not only

to Rachel, but his patients, his staff, his colleagues…and anyone else understanding and kind enough to listen. Juggling career and parenting responsibilities was an overwhelming task. One at which he was sure he was failing miserably.

"I'm just teasing you." Rachel shifted Joy onto one arm and then held up a crisp white lab coat for Greg with her free hand. "It's only been a week. Give yourself time."

He slipped on the coat and fastened the buttons with swift, precise movements. "So many times this week I've wished Mom and Dad were alive to help me. They'd have loved Joy so much." He sighed. I can't believe I'm having such a devil of a time finding a sitter. It's ridiculous. No one wants to watch Joy at home. I don't think it's a good idea to take her to a day-care center. She'll have a constant cold if she's with other children."

Rachel shook her head. "Greg, millions of mothers and fathers drop off their children at day cares all over the country every single day. Joy would be with other kids. Think of the social skills she'd develop." She handed him his stethoscope and then his first patient's file. "You're going to have to do *something*. I'm an office manager," she reminded him gently, "not a nanny."

"I know, I know." Apology was in his tone, deep and sincere—Rachel had been a godsend this past week—but suddenly his whole countenance brightened as what she'd said really sunk into his head.

"A nanny." He let the word roll around on his tongue, roll around in his mind. "That's just what I need."

"Oh." Rachel waved off the idea. "You don't want someone living with you night and day."

"But I've got plenty of room," Greg said. "My apartment has three bedrooms."

"Your whole life would be disrupted."

He cocked one brow at her. "Like it hasn't been already?"

She laughed. And they were both rewarded when little Joy joined in.

"Ah—" Greg smoothed a finger along his daughter's satiny jaw "—you liked that one, huh? You like knowing you've thrown your daddy for a loop?"

The toddler's bubbly giggle made Greg chuckle. He'd taken quite a shine to her during the one short week she'd spent under his roof.

"This little girl is just too charming." Rachel touched the end of Joy's tiny, button nose, then leveled her gaze on Greg. "Too bad her dad couldn't muster up any charisma this morning."

Greg let his silence urge the office manager to expound on her comment.

"You couldn't find your razor?" she asked.

Of its own volition, his hand reached up to cup his jaw. "Oh, Lord. I never gave it a thought."

Merriment danced in Rachel's eyes. "This daddy business really has rocked your world right off its axis, hasn't it?"

Rather than responding, he took a second to glance down at himself. His tie was askew and his belt was fastened but hadn't been tucked into the last loop.

"I feel like I've been through an earthquake." Then he amended, "A daily earthquake. She's pretty good during the days. But the nights…'' He sighed wearily. "She still cries for her mother at bedtime. I've got to rock her and sing to her for hours before she'll fall asleep.''

Rachel offered a compassionate smile. "It'll get easier. I promise. But right now, you'd better get to that patient. She's been waiting a good while.''

"Of course.'' However, before he left the waiting area, he tickled Joy under the chin and was rewarded with her sunny grin. He'd had no idea a man could lose his heart so thoroughly in just seven short days.

Jane sat on the examining table, her stomach dancing with a horrible case of nerves. She shouldn't be here. She didn't have a plan. This impulsiveness just wasn't like her. But she *had* to find Joy. Her heart felt aching and empty without that baby in her life. How could Pricilla just disappear with the child like she had? How could her sister do such a thing?

Hot tears prickled the backs of Jane's eyelids when she thought of her niece with her huge jewel-green eyes, her springy red curls and those deep dimples that formed every time the child grinned. Jane dashed the moisture away with a quick swipe of her fingertips. She couldn't afford tears. Not now. She had to try to keep her wits about her. Dr. Greg Hamilton would be arriving any moment.

She glanced at the white clock on the wall. He was late. But could she expect anything else from the haphazard and irresponsible man who had made her sister pregnant and then would have nothing else to do with her or the baby he'd created?

Tamp down that anger, she warned herself. Giving

Greg Hamilton a piece of her mind would be satisfying, yes. But it would get her nowhere in locating Pricilla and Joy. And that was the sole reason she was here.

A whole week had passed since she'd arrived home from the restaurant where she worked as a waitress to find the apartment empty. Pricilla had left no note. No hint of where she'd gone or when she planned to return. At first, Jane had been furious, thinking that her sister had taken the baby with her on a date, or something equally as capricious.

Pricilla was always doing things on a whim. She never thought her actions through. And that unguarded attitude often placed her own baby in neglectful circumstances. Hadn't Jane just argued with Pricilla about that very subject two days before her sister and niece disappeared?

Jane had discovered that, rather than staying home with Joy while Jane was at work, Pricilla had been leaving the baby with a neighbor—a young woman neither of them knew very well—and going out on the town. Jane hated to admit it, but her sister's maternal instinct wasn't very strong. It had been sheer luck that Jane had beat her sister home by a mere five minutes and caught her fetching Joy from the house down the block. The hour had been late, and the baby had been wearing nothing but her pajamas to ward off the late October chill.

Jane and Pricilla had an awful argument about the incident. Money was so tight. Jane hadn't even asked where Pricilla had gotten the funds to pay the neighbor for baby-sitting. Probably from the big-spending men-friends she dated...the ones who seemed to crawl out of the woodwork whenever Pricilla had it in her mind to go out and party. Men who thought nothing of their actions. Men whose only concern was having a good time.

Men like Greg Hamilton.

The name hadn't even finished whispering across her brain when the door of the examining room opened and the man himself appeared before her.

Jane's eyes widened, and at the same time her heart skittered into a race. The man was too darned handsome for words! But then, did Pricilla ever choose any other kind?

"Hello."

He smiled after he spoke, and Jane knew without a doubt from whom baby Joy inherited her dimples. However, while her niece's were cute enough to invoke grins, the deep indentations in Greg Hamilton's cheeks were…breathtaking. Even shadowed with a day's growth of auburn whiskers, those dimples were absolutely mesmerizing. And his eyes were as green as little Joy's, too.

"Hi." Her greeting sounded whispery, halting. She silently berated herself. What did she care if his damned dimples made him look like some Hollywood movie star? Or if his eyes glittered attractively? She was appalled by the way her heart skipped and scampered against her ribs, the way her stomach constricted at the sight of him.

"I'm Dr. Hamilton."

He reached out for her hand and she automatically clasped his. His palm was warm against hers. Secure. Trustworthy. Just like a doctor's hand should be. Again, he smiled. And again, her insides went utterly haywire. The spontaneous and downright shocking feelings she was experiencing toward this man were so at odds with the opinion she'd formed of him that she felt sure her brain would short-circuit at any moment.

"Jane," she told him, relieved that she'd even remembered her name. "Jane Dale."

"Nice to meet you." Then he said, "Give me a moment to look at your file and then you can tell me what I can do for you today." He went to the counter and flipped open the manila folder he'd carried in with him.

She was happy to give him as long as he needed. The way things were going, she needed some time herself. Time to bridle these unexpected and totally confusing emotions that were wreaking havoc on her nervous system.

The giddiness was purely a feminine response to a good-looking man. That much, she knew, was completely natural. Completely controllable. But why was she angry that Greg Hamilton was handsome? She had expected him to be, hadn't she? Pricilla wouldn't have been caught dead with a man who didn't have above average looks.

You're angry because men like the good doctor here, a tiny, hurtful voice silently intoned, *would never find you attractive.*

That was ludicrous! She didn't give a hoot if Greg Hamilton, or any other man for that matter, found her attractive or not.

What did anger her were the facts. This man fathered a baby and then refused to have anything to do with the child unless he could have full custody.

This man had refused to help Pricilla when he certainly had the means to do so. He'd refused to support his daughter. Those were the facts. Facts that made Jane smolder like a day-old bonfire.

Stay calm, she scolded herself. If she lambasted him like she wanted to—*like he deserved*—he would surely refuse to help her find Pricilla and Joy.

Why would he help you, anyway? that irritating voice silently taunted. Pricilla had said early on that Dr. Hamilton wanted full custody of his daughter, or he wanted nothing to do with the child. Discovering that Pricilla had suddenly gone off with Joy just might stir in him a renewed interest in his baby girl.

Jane felt the blood drain right out of her face.

What if he decided to take Joy away from Pricilla? What if he hired a lawyer? What if he demanded his rights as the baby's father be recognized? Her mind whirred faster than the speed of light.

Why hadn't she thought of all these things before she'd come here? Why hadn't she realized that she was entering enemy territory? This kind of thoughtless, irresponsible behavior was usually carried out by her sister, not level-headed Jane. But now Jane herself was being swept away by some insane recklessness.

She could be causing Pricilla trouble just by being here. Seeking him out. *Jane could lose Joy for good.*

That final thought caused her to tremble, literally. Perspiration prickled her forehead and upper lip. She felt light-headed. Dizzy. A frown bit deeply into her brow as she contemplated the magnitude of the mistake she'd made in coming to see Greg Hamilton. But it was too late now. Too late to get out of here without starting some kind of trouble. For Pricilla. For herself.

You can get out of this, a stern, no-nonsense voice echoed in her head. *All you have to do is lie. You've already set it up perfectly.*

In her reluctance to reveal the true purpose of her visit to anyone except Greg Hamilton himself, she had told the receptionist and the nurse she was here for a physical. All she had to do was stick with that story. This would be simple. A piece of cake, really.

She thanked her lucky stars that she and Pricilla had different fathers, hence different last names. The doctor didn't know her. Had never met her. So there was no reason why he would link the mousy-haired woman sitting in his examining room now with the blond, blue-eyed, gorgeous bombshell that was Pricilla. The logical voice in her head made getting out of this situation unscathed sound so terribly easy.

Nervously running her tongue over her dry lips, Jane tried to make sense of these rash, chaotic thoughts.

Lying is for cheats and swindlers, another part of her brain argued.

Not all liars were bad, the stern voice stressed. *Look at poets and song writers, novelists and playwrights. They fabricated stories every single day. They made up people, places, events.*

But that was solely for entertainment purposes, her rational side reasoned.

No, the stern voice pointed out, *it was for survival. And that's just what you need to do right now. Survive. So you'd better lie like there's no tomorrow.*

* * *

Greg leaned his weight on one elbow, his forehead in his hand, and stared unseeingly at the medical history page in front of him. The woman's blood pressure was fine. Her weight was perfect for her height. Yet he still continued to stare at the page.

As inconspicuously as possible, he inhaled a huge breath of air, and then expelled it slowly. When he'd entered the room and looked into Jane Dale's face, it was as if he'd been kicked in the chest by a mule. She seemed so…haunted. He was almost positive her ailment wasn't physical.

Her gray-blue eyes were clouded. Intense. *Desperate.*

It didn't take a medical degree to clearly see that she'd had at least one sleepless night. And from the look of the dark smudges on the porcelain skin under her eyes, she hadn't slept well for days. Something deep inside him stirred.

Instinct had urged him to reach for her, hug her to him. Give her the comfort she so obviously needed. However, that would have been behavior of the most unprofessional kind. So he'd made an excuse out of studying the few facts he had about her. Height. Weight. Blood pressure. Temperature.

Truth was, he needed to put some space between them. To get a grip on himself. His reaction to Jane Dale had taken him completely by surprise.

He was sure his new attitude about women was to blame. He'd really been shaken when Pricilla had shown up with Joy. The past week with his daughter had been hard. Oh, boy, had it ever been! But being a father had also been like having a small piece of heaven dropped right into his lap.

Yet, it was the situation—his having made Pricilla pregnant over a year and a half ago and him without a clue that it had happened—that had totally altered his thinking where women were concerned. Had he really been so callous, so careless, that he could have made a woman pregnant and not known about it? His whole outlook on life had been shattered.

He gave the woman a surreptitious glance, wondering what on earth was troubling her. Only one way to find out. Straightening his spine, he turned to face her. "So what can I do for you today?"

"A physical."

Her answer was rushed, her tone curt, and that made Greg all the more intrigued by this delicate-looking woman.

He automatically reached for his stethoscope. "Have you been feeling okay lately?"

"Oh, yes," she assured him. "I'm not sick or anything. But I need a physical." Almost as an afterthought, she quickly added, "For a job."

"Ah, so you're starting a new job." A little doctor-patient dialogue might help him find out something about her, something about her life-style…her troubles.

"Well…" She hesitated. "I don't have a job yet. I'm new in town. But I plan to be working soon. I've got to be. To pay for a place to live. The hotel where I'm staying isn't cheap."

He smiled. "Welcome to Philadelphia. What type of job are you looking for?"

As he spoke, he moved toward her with the metallic diaphragm of the stethoscope outstretched. And he was taken aback when she leaned away from him.

"I just need to take a quick listen to your heart and lungs," he explained, hoping to put her at ease.

Those huge cloud-gray eyes of hers slid away from his gaze, but she remained still while he slipped the diaphragm between the facings of her blouse and pressed it to her chest.

Her skin was like warm satin against his fingertips, and the lacy edge of her bra had him averting his own gaze toward the far corner of the small cubicle.

What was the matter with him? He caught glimpses of people's underclothing all day long. Seeing a bit of lace during an examination had never flustered him before. But he was sure flustered now. In fact, he was so disconcerted by his reaction to this woman that he hoped his hands didn't begin to shake. This was crazy!

Occupy your mind. Let routine take over.

Conversation. That's what he needed. Get lost in some small talk.

He realized then that she hadn't answered his question regarding what kind of job she was seeking.

"I see you as...maybe...an elementary schoolteacher?"

Jane Dale actually smiled at his out-of-the-blue guess, and her whole face was transformed by the expression. The edges of her mouth softened. Even the anxiety in her gaze seemed to relent just a little.

She was pretty. In a natural kind of way. A natural beauty. That's how Greg would describe her.

However, rather than taking note of her looks, he knew he should be focusing on her physical health. Period.

"I do love kids," she said wistfully. "But I'm not a teacher."

"A photographer, then," he suggested. "Or a bank manager. A nurse. A cement truck driver?"

"A what?" There was laughter in her voice, despite whatever turmoil was plaguing her.

Greg thought he'd never heard a more beautiful sound. "Hey, this is a new millennium. Women can do and be whatever they want."

Her smile faltered. "Well...if you say so."

There it was again. That haunted expression shadowing those unusual gray-blue eyes.

Pressing his fingers to either side of her long, slender throat, he felt the left and right lobes of her thyroid gland, and at the same time he wondered what it would be like to press his lips against the silky length of her neck. The thought made his heart trip in his chest.

"So what *do* you want to be when you grow up," he asked, his tone unwittingly dropping to a soft murmur as he forced the sexy image of him kissing her from his mind's eye.

"Does that really matter? What I *am* is a plain old waitress."

There's nothing plain or old about you, Jane Dale. I just wish I could get into your head. Find out what it is that's troubling you so.

The thoughts came out of nowhere and nearly made him step back away from her. But he quelled the reaction and made yet another silent vow to keep these very inappropriate thoughts at bay.

Being a doctor often meant more than simply finding a cure for his patient's physical ills. Often, he had to delve into a person's psyche. Get into the mind to try to discover what worries might be harrying a person and adding to their suffering.

What was so confusing about what he was experiencing at this moment was the strange mixture of intrigue, curiosity and...attraction. Yes, attraction.

He knew very well that his confusion was caused by the change in his attitude. Ever since Pricilla showed up on his doorstep with Joy, he'd been beating himself up for taking women for granted. It was this transformation in his thinking that had him so...mesmerized. So intrigued by Jane Dale and whatever was so obviously bothering her. That's what was behind this discombobulated reaction he was experiencing.

"I'd like to be able to say that I have a teaching certificate," she told him. "Or that I'm certified as a nurse. Or trained as a photographer." She sighed. "But my only claim to fame is that I'm pretty good at slinging hash."

Jane Dale had a sense of humor. Greg grinned. He liked the woman.

He found himself murmuring, "It's too bad you're not a Mary Poppins type."

She went utterly still. "I beg your pardon?"

"Oh, you know, a governess. An au pair. A nanny." Absently, Greg reached up and rubbed his fingers over his day's growth of beard and thought about just how badly he needed help at home with Joy. "If you had experience with children, I just might have a job for you."

Hell, he couldn't say why he'd make such an offer. He didn't even know this woman. But thoughts of Joy, of the sleepless nights he'd had, of the seemingly endless piles of baby clothes waiting at home to be laundered, added with Rachel's complaint just a few minutes ago that she was an office manager and not a baby-sitter...all these things had him speaking before he really had time to think about what he was saying. Jane was a nice woman. A healthy woman. He'd just checked that out, hadn't he? He smiled to himself. And he liked her. Besides that, she needed a job.

"Oh? You need someone…"

He chuckled. "But, of course, being a waitress, you're not going to be interested in changing diapers and finding ways to make a baby girl eat strained peas."

"A-a b-baby girl?"

Greg nodded. "I have a brand-new baby." Then he said, "Well, not brand-new. Joy is ten months old. She's cute as a button. And best of all, she's got my dimples." He smiled big and pointed to his cheeks.

Okay, so he was a proud daddy. Jane Dale would just have to understand.

"Y-you need a sitter?"

"Actually, I was thinking of live-in help. Like a—" he shrugged "—a nanny. But you probably wouldn't be interested, seeing as how your experience is in food services."

"Wait." Her voice sounded small, almost uncertain. "I do have experience with children. I, um, I just came from living with my sister. She's got a baby. And I handled, well, I handled most all of the child care. When I wasn't working at my job at the restaurant, that is.''

Greg was amazed that she would even consider his suggestion. He hadn't really expected anything to come of the offer.

"Wow. This is great." He moistened his lips, reality sinking in. "Could I meet her? Your sister, I mean? Or could you at least supply some kind of..." He felt like a heel for asking, but couldn't help himself. This was his daughter they were talking about. "Um, letter of recommendation?"

"Sure."

He watched her throat convulse with what looked like a nervous swallow. Apprehension fairly pulsed from her. A blaring hint of just how badly she must need a job.

"I'll get my sister to write a glowing recommendation. And—and I'll even get her to stop in the next time she's down this way."

She frowned and nibbled on her bottom lip, and Greg had to drag his gaze from her mouth.

"Would that be sufficient?" she asked.

Something made him pause. He was rushing into this. And maybe he shouldn't be. But for the first time since he'd come into the room and made this woman's acquaintance, the shadows cleared from her gaze.

He'd lifted the worry from her shoulders. That made him feel pretty darned good, even if he did say so himself.

His head bobbed and he grinned at her. "That will

be great.'' He shook her hand, then caught her attention with raised brows. ''Do you have any qualms about starting immediately? As in, this very second?''

Chapter Two

"**Y**ou did *what?*"

Sloan Radcliff, the older of Greg's two partners, stared at Greg, disbelief and disapproval darkening his countenance like a storm cloud.

Greg leaned his elbows on the counter of the office's waiting room. All the patients were gone, the staff, too, and the partners had just happened to meet up at the end of this long day.

"I hired a nanny for Joy. What's so bad about that?"

With his brows raised high, Sloan continued to censure Greg's actions with a small shake of his head.

Travis Westcott, Greg's other partner, stood just behind Sloan and obviously couldn't find the words to even respond to this surprising turn of events.

"This woman might have made a good impression on you this morning, Greg," Sloan said. "But she's still a stranger. You know nothing about her. And you're trusting her to care for your baby girl.''

Greg couldn't tell if this last sentence was a statement or a question. And the doubt his friend tossed out affected him mightily. Maybe he had jumped into this too quickly.

The manner in which he'd become a father—so out of the blue—had Greg leaning on his buddies a great deal this past week. And Sloan and Travis had come through for him with plenty of advice and support. He respected their opinions. And it was clear that Sloan didn't think very highly of his decision to hire Jane on the spot this morning.

''Well, I was pretty desperate for some help,'' Greg said, knowing his words made him sound defensive. Why shouldn't they? He *was* on the defensive. ''You should have seen Joy's eyes light up at the sight of Jane. It was like they were old friends or something. Joy took to Jane like a duck to water. It was amazing, I tell you.''

He shifted his weight onto the other foot. ''I stopped in at the house unannounced today at lunch. And Jane was doing great with Joy. They were playing with blocks. Making little stacks and knocking them down in the middle of the living room floor. And Jane had already dived into that mountain of laundry. And the kitchen sink was free of dirty dishes for the first time all week. The beds were made. The toys picked up. And she'd done all this in just a couple of hours. When I get home, I just may discover that she's given the whole apartment complex an overhaul.'' His hollow laughter died quickly when his friends didn't join in. His brow wrinkled in a pitiful frown. "Look, guys, I *need* the woman. I need her help. Try to understand."

Travis and Sloan just looked at him, and Greg surrendered to the welling urge to try again to convince his friends that what he was doing was the right thing for him and his daughter.

"Look," he said passionately, "you guys know that I was happy to take Joy from Pricilla. I want to be responsible for my actions. And I have every intention of being a good father to my daughter for the rest of my life."

The stern-lipped disapproval on the other men's faces softened.

"But single parents can't do it alone," he continued. "Sloan, as the father of triplets, you should know that. You get a sitter for the girls once every couple of weeks. You go out. You have a good time. And you have a housekeeper, too, to help you with the cooking and cleaning. I can't do this alone."

Greg hated the accusatory tone he used. He hated throwing up into Sloan's face any fun the man might have. Sloan, the father of nearly teen triplet girls, was a widower—a widower who was still grieving almost two years after losing his wife. But Greg was being bested by the desperation he felt to make his friends comprehend his plight.

"Yes," Sloan agreed quietly, "I do get a sitter every now and then. But only so that I can have a beer with you two after work. I never stay out late. And I always get home in plenty of time to tuck my girls into bed."

Guilt solidified in the pit of Greg's stomach. He hadn't the right to make his friend feel the need to defend himself like this. But before he could apologize, he discovered Sloan had more to say.

"And I do have a housekeeper. With three preteens running rampant in my house, I'd be a lunatic not to." Sloan ran his finger absently along the corner of the counter as if he was debating how to word what was on his mind. Finally, he said, "But there's a big difference between having a housekeeper come in a few times a week and having live-in help. Especially when you just met this woman." He raised his eyes, locking gazes with Greg. "I'm going to say something you're not going to like."

Instant wariness had Greg steeling himself.

His friend sighed. "Travis and I both know that this past week has been hard on you. Dealing with fatherhood has really thrown a monkey wrench into the cogs of your life. And we also realize that finding out about Joy…finding out that a casual affair you had made you a dad…has, ah—" he stammered for the first time "—done something radical to your thinking."

"Now, wait just a minute—"

"This has to be said," Travis softly interrupted, the step he took closer to Sloan clear evidence that he agreed with whatever revelation the man was about to make.

Sloan plowed ahead. "You've taken this woman into your home—"

"Her name's Jane," Greg said, his hackles rising. "Jane Dale."

"Okay, Jane Dale." This time when Sloan continued, his tone was gentler. "I think your hiring her has a great deal to do with what happened to you.

Your thinking about women has become…confused. You think you can save this woman. This Jane. You found out she was needy. So you gave her a job and a place to live. You're somehow trying to make up for your behavior in the past."

This was the truth. Greg had known it. He'd thought that very thing himself this morning when he was examining Jane in his office, hadn't he? But why did his motivation for hiring Jane sound so blasted *twisted* coming from someone else's mouth?

"We want you to know," Travis added, "that we don't believe you've done anything to make up for. It's not a crime to date women. Pricilla was a consenting adult, right? And it's your habit to practice safe sex, right?" Lifting his hand, palm up, Travis said, "Mistakes happen. Yes, you have to take responsibility for your actions. And you're doing that. But you don't have to try to save the world."

But I never called Pricilla, the silent lamentation screeched across Greg's mind like fingernails on a blackboard. *I never reached out to her afterward. If I had, I'd have found out about my daughter sooner. All I thought about was getting away from a bad situation. All I thought about was myself.*

Shoving the thoughts aside, he decided not to allow himself to get sidetracked with these dark recriminations regarding what he should have done. He needed to stick to the topic at hand.

"B-but," he stuttered lamely, "I'm not just helping Jane. She's helping me, too." Then he let his eyes slide from one friend to the other. "Do you guys really think I'm a nutcase for hiring her?"

Both men remained silent for a moment. Travis

shifted his overstuffed briefcase from one hand to the other. Then leveled a steady gaze at Greg.

"My friend," Travis said, "just think about what you've done, and how out of sorts it seems with your usual actions. When we wanted to hire a new nurse for the practice, you refused to let the woman near the patients until we had three letters of recommendation from her previous employers. *Three.* Like Sloan said, you don't know this Jane Dale." He bit his bottom lip a moment. Quietly, he pointed out, "This is your daughter we're talking about. *Your daughter.*"

A cold shiver clawed its way up Greg's spine as revelation struck. "And I've left her with a complete stranger all day. A woman I know nothing about."

Without another word, Greg snatched up his valise and headed for the front door.

Jane could not believe her good fortune. She'd actually lied her way into a job as Joy's nanny. She was once again with the light of her life. Nothing could have made her happier.

When she'd arrived in town, she'd had no idea what she meant to do other than to throw herself on Greg Hamilton's mercy, beg him for information about where Pricilla and Joy might be. During the days since her sister had disappeared with the baby, Jane had called every friend Pricilla had ever talked about. When a week had passed with no word from her sister, Jane felt she simply couldn't hang around the apartment any longer. She wasn't eating. Wasn't sleeping. Couldn't keep her mind on her work. She'd reached the end of her rope. She simply *had* to find

Joy. However, when Jane had gone to her boss to ask for some time off to search for her family, she'd been told that if she walked out the door, she'd be walking away from her job. For good.

Jane had walked out the door without a backward glance.

She'd been that desperate to find her niece. She'd been that desperate to somehow heal the aching hole the baby's disappearance had left in her heart. In her soul. She'd been that desperate to put to rest the worry she'd felt for Joy's welfare. Pricilla had proved time and again during the past ten months that she wasn't a good mother. Heck, Pricilla hadn't wanted Joy. Who knew what her sister might do? Jane had been terribly anxious for Joy's well-being.

Once she'd left her job, Jane had visited all Pricilla's friends, hoping against hope that one of them had lied about harboring her sister and niece. Jane had questioned each of them. None of them had known where Pricilla might be. A few of them had told Jane that surely Pricilla would show up. Eventually.

Jane couldn't take that chance. Not with Joy's health and safety at stake.

It might have sounded strange, but little Joy always seemed to feel discomfited by her own mother's presence. The baby would fidget and cry and reach for Jane. Jane suspected the child sensed Pricilla's lack of mothering instinct.

To be absolutely honest, Jane loved Joy as if she were her own daughter. She *felt* like Joy's mother. She loved the child to distraction. And that's why she was willing to give up everything in order to find her.

And she had!

Jane had hardly believed her ears when the doctor mentioned needing a nanny for his daughter. She'd nearly toppled right off the examining table onto the floor.

Images of her appointment with Dr. Greg Hamilton this morning swirled, unbidden, into her brain like the heated waters of some tropic flood, invading and filling every nook and cranny of her thoughts. His hands had been so warm, so gentle on her skin as he'd listened to her heartbeat. She'd been certain that her pulse had accelerated. And she'd been utterly mortified when the silky touch of his fingers brushing her chest had caused her nipples to bud to life. However, she'd noticed that his gaze had been averted, and for that she'd been terribly relieved. Even now, as she thought about the way his mahogany hair fell in thick waves, the way his forest-green eyes studied her with concern, her heartbeat pounded, her face flushed.

"Stop." She whispered the word aloud and Joy looked up at her from where she sat on the floor, gnawing happily on a teething ring.

How Joy came to be in Greg's care, Jane couldn't be sure. But there could only be one answer. Pricilla had given the baby to Greg.

Jane had no idea if Pricilla planned to return for Joy. Or if her sister simply meant to give Greg all parental rights to the baby.

The mere idea made Jane tremble with fear. She

couldn't imagine her life without this baby in it. She just couldn't.

The lies she'd told Greg were wrong. She'd known that even as the grand stories had come rushing from her. However, she had good cause. And she reached for that cause, a big smile spreading across her face.

"Are you ready for a bath?" Jane asked Joy.

Joy chuckled, the dimples in her creamy cheeks deepening. The baby was so happy with any small amount of attention she received. Joy was an angel. She was Jane's angel. It was true that Jane hadn't given birth to this little girl, but she couldn't love the child more even if she had.

"Let's go have a tubby," Jane crooned.

She'd have to tell Greg the truth. She knew that. But she'd win his trust first. She'd show him that she was the mother for Joy that Pricilla simply didn't have it in her to be.

As she gathered together a towel, the baby shampoo and a washcloth, she felt her whole abdomen seize with icy dread. She had no legal claim on Joy. She couldn't fight Greg for custody. Not when she was only the baby's aunt. No court of law would side with her. And it seemed that Pricilla had lost all interest in helping her raise Joy.

Hot tears blurred Jane's vision as she plugged up the drain of the kitchen's big porcelain sink and turned on the spigot. Joy reached up and tweaked Jane's bottom lip between her chubby fingers, seeming to sense her melancholy mood.

"It's okay," Jane said. And she didn't know whether her words were meant more to assure the baby or herself. Then she whispered, "It really is going to be okay."

She was with Joy. And for the moment, that was going to have to be enough.

Joy was still splashing in the warm water of the sink when Jane heard Greg come in through the front door.

"Hello? Jane? Where are you?"

The frantic tone of the doctor's voice had her frowning. Something was wrong. Something terrible. Goose bumps rose on her arms as some kind of intrinsic proof.

Leaving the baby unattended wasn't an option, so she called out, "We're in here. In the kitchen."

He literally burst through the doorway.

"What?" The anxiety pulsing from him frightened Jane and she reached for Joy with both hands, pulling her from the sink and clutching the baby's wet body to her, heedless of the water dribbling down her clothing. "What's the matter?"

The sight of them seemed to assuage the apprehension that darkened his green eyes.

"I was just...worried."

She didn't like his tone. Or his frown. Or the way he was looking at her. This morning—and then again when he'd come home at lunchtime—he had been so confident in her, so at ease with the idea that she was caring for Joy, so relieved to have her help.

"You see," he continued in a rush to explain his abrupt arrival, "I was feeling a little nervous. It's been quite a while since lunch and...and this is your first day with Joy and all."

Trepidation had Jane's gaze narrowing. Something

had happened to cause this anxiety in him. And it must have to do with her. He was obviously having second thoughts about hiring her.

Greg went to the counter, picked up the towel and wrapped it around his daughter. His fingertips pressed against Jane's shoulder, her arm, her waist, every place that he tucked the towel around Joy's little body.

"You're getting soaked."

His tone was calmer now, and it smoothed over her like warm velvet. Jane's throat went dry, a giddy feeling rose up in her chest and she blinked several times. She wished her body wouldn't react to him, to his touch, to his voice, so...wildly.

Thankfully, he was distracted by Joy's smile of greeting—a smile that turned into a delighted giggle at the sight of her daddy.

"Hey, little girl," he said softly. "Did you miss me today?"

He went to take Joy from Jane.

"But you'll get your suit all wet," Jane warned.

"It's okay." Joy went to him, gladly. "It's only water. It'll dry."

He gave his daughter a soft kiss on the forehead. The gesture was sweet enough to make Jane smile. She didn't want to like Greg Hamilton. She wanted him to be the ogre she'd conjured him to be in her mind. But that image was fading fast. It was obvious that he cared about his little girl.

But he refused to help Pricilla unless she signed over full custody. This man is too controlling. Heartlessly so.

Jane pushed aside the silent arguments for and

against him. She needed to focus on the here and now.

"Why don't you take her into her room?" she suggested. "I was just going to get her ready for bed."

She led the way down the hall, and Greg made delightful baby conversation with his daughter as he followed. The sound of it made Jane grin even though an uneasiness was swirling in her belly.

"You know—" he sat Joy on the changing table and dried her with the towel "—it's a good thing I came straight home. Bedtime is a nightmare around here. This little girl cries herself to sleep every night. It's usually a three-hour ordeal. You might be sorry you got yourself into this."

"Oh, no." Jane smiled to herself as she searched through the dresser drawer for pajama top and bottom. She quietly added, "I'll never be sorry. That's for sure."

He set the towel aside and eased Joy down so he could place a diaper on her bottom. "You really didn't have any problems today? She took a nap for you? Ate her lunch?"

"Not a single tear," she told him. "All day long. She ate some rice cereal for lunch. A little applesauce. And drank a bottle of milk. Then she napped for more than an hour."

Jane approached the changing table and tickled Joy's belly. "You were a perfect little angel weren't you, my Joy?"

Suddenly, Jane froze. Had she acted too familiar with her niece? Would Greg realize she was no stranger to this baby?

"She is an angel, isn't she?"

Greg's easy manner made her want to sigh with relief. Her expression was stiff as she looked up at him.

"Yes, she is."

She busied herself tucking one of Joy's feet into the leg of the cotton pajama bottom.

"Jane."

He paused. He swallowed. And Jane knew he was about to say something she wasn't going to like.

"I've been thinking," he continued. "Maybe we, um, jumped into this, ah, arrangement too quickly."

"No way." She waved off his remark, keeping her tone airy and light, then reached to pull the elastic-waist pants over Joy's little bottom. But fear lumped in her throat. He was going to fire her just when she'd found Joy. He was going to ask her to leave his home just when she'd been reunited with her little girl. She couldn't let that happen. She couldn't!

"Don't you worry about me," she told him. "I'm just fine. I told you, Joy and I made out great together today. We played. We laughed. I read to her. And I cleaned the house." Her words came tumbling from her tongue in a rush. "I washed clothes. I cleaned up the kitchen. I picked up. And…" She paused to take a deep breath, sitting Joy up and dressing her in the pajama top. The last thing she wanted was to sound too desperate. That might make Greg ill at ease. "I cooked dinner. I saved you a plate. It's ready to be reheated in the microwave."

She lifted Joy onto her hip, then tucked her bottom lip between her teeth. Taking a deep inhalation, she tried to control the fear that had a tight grip on her. Finally, she glanced up at Greg. "Please give me a chance."

A frown dug deeply into his brow. "It's not you," he said. "You've done a great job. And I do appreciate it." His head tilted a fraction. "It's me."

Joy squirmed to get down onto the floor among her toys, so Jane put the baby down and moved some blocks within her reach. Then she straightened her spine and looked at Greg.

"I was talking with my friends this evening," he said. "Both Sloan and Travis feel that…I might have rushed into this situation. And after having some time to think it over—" his full, sexy lips pursed for a moment before he finally admitted "—I'm afraid I might have to agree with them."

They stared at each other, he obviously feeling guilty, she feeling tremendously desperate. She didn't want to be tossed out on her ear. She wanted to be here. With Joy. She had to do something. Say something that would make him change his mind.

"Do your friends believe I'm a serial killer, or something?" She chuckled, hoping to break the tension with humor. But when she thought about some of the outlandish national news stories she'd read and heard on radio and TV in the past, this suggestion of hers didn't sound so funny. Stranger things happened every single day in these times.

"Greg, please." Her expression as well as her tone revealed the utter sincerity she felt. "I know I'm pretty much a stranger to you. But I want this job. I *need* it."

What an understatement that was, she thought.

"I know you don't know me," she continued. "Your friends don't know me. But all of you can *get* to know me…if you'll just give me a chance."

Indecision flickered in his gaze. She could clearly see it, and it gave her hope.

"I'm not terribly educated," she admitted. "I had to drop out of college in my freshman year. But I am well read. I've worked hard all my life. Supported myself. And my sister. So I'm hard-working. I always have been." Her tone went all whispery as she automatically added, "I was forced to be."

Uneasiness crept over every inch of her skin. She hadn't meant to reveal this much personal information about herself. Before he could ask her to elaborate, she softly blurted. "I'm dependable. And honest."

These things were true…well, usually they were, but remembering the lies she'd conjured for Greg this morning, the withholding of information and her true relationship to Joy, Jane nearly choked when that adjective had slipped from her lips.

In a rush, she added, "I'm good-hearted…I'm trustworthy…I'm simple and straightforward.…"

She flushed to the roots of her hair. As complicated as this mess was that she'd created, her life was turning into something that was the exact opposite of simple and straightforward.

"Look." Her gaze was beseeching, pleading, and she knew it. "I'm capable. And I'll work hard. I'll take good care of Joy. I will. Just give me a chance."

He studied her for a long, silent moment. Finally, he heaved a sigh. "I'm sorry. But until you can give me some references…"

A lump rose up in Jane's throat, and tears burned her eye sockets. She pressed her lips together tightly to keep her chin from trembling.

A single, hot and desperate tear trailed slowly down her cheek. She couldn't have stopped it if she'd tried.

"Please don't cry," he said. "You said you could provide references. You can get them over the weekend. As soon as I look them over, we'll discuss the job again. Next week."

She wasn't normally a crier. She didn't allow life to get the best of her. The road of her life had been rocky a time or two. Or three. However, she wasn't the kind of person to wallow in self-pity. But she hated the idea of walking out Greg Hamilton's door and leaving Joy behind just when she'd found the baby again.

Oh, why hadn't she just been up-front with him from the beginning?

Because he's the enemy, a stern voice intoned in her head.

But he seemed too darned nice to be anyone's enemy.

This man is a stranger to you, the voice chided. *Just as you are a stranger to him. Pricilla's told you enough about him to let you know you cannot trust him with the truth.*

He had turned his back on Pricilla. He had refused to offer his daughter monetary support unless he was granted sole custody. Those were the facts. And a man who was *that* controlling would never allow Jane to care for Joy if he knew she was the sister of the woman who had given birth to his daughter.

"Please." Her whisper was husky and paper-dry to her own ears.

"I'm sorry, honey."

He meant the nickname as a comfort, she knew. But all she felt was desolation, humiliation. And anger.

She was angry with herself for getting into this mess. She was angry with herself for not standing up to Joy's father.

But what good would it do? None. Somehow, he'd gotten his hands on her niece. And until she found Pricilla, until she discovered whether or not Greg meant to keep Joy, she really couldn't do anything but surrender to his whims and wishes.

A shaky sigh expelled from her lips, and she nodded. "Okay," she told him. "I'll go." She paused, one last spark of an idea coming into her head, an idea that would make it possible for her to have just a few more minutes with Joy. "But would you mind if I put her to bed? It wouldn't take long. And then I'll go."

Greg shook his head. "I don't believe that would be wise. It's an awful chore, anyway, what with all the tears and all. You go get your things together. And we'll talk again. Next week."

She gave him a slow, resigned nod. And then she walked out of the baby's bedroom.

Chapter Three

The baby's cries continued for every one of the seventeen minutes it took Jane to slowly and reluctantly gather the clothes she'd unpacked earlier and tuck them neatly into her small carryall. She checked her watch every thirty seconds or so, mentally battling the urge to go and comfort her niece. The hallway bathroom was directly opposite Joy's room, so when Jane went to retrieve her makeup case and personal effects from the marble countertop, the toddler's sobbing was even more audible, more soulwrenching.

Jane was sure her heart was going to rip right in two. She couldn't leave Joy. Not like this. Not with her crying and upset.

Greg had mentioned that bedtime for Joy was a nightmare, Jane remembered on her way back toward her bedroom. But it didn't have to be. Not if she were allowed to rock her niece to sleep.

Finally, she could take it no longer. Tossing her small makeup case on the bed beside her suitcase, Jane turned around and headed back toward the baby's room.

She knocked on the door, and without waiting for an answer, she pushed her way into the room. Greg look flustered and helpless.

"Here," she said, hustling over to the two of them, "let me take care of this." Maybe if she just bullied her way into helping him, he wouldn't have a chance to reject her offer.

She scooped Joy up with both her arms, and the baby immediately hugged her tight, stuck a pink thumb into her mouth and rested her head on Jane's shoulder.

All was quiet.

Jane's ploy worked. Greg's expression clearly revealed that he'd been steamrollered. He sat in the rocker, blinking, gaping up at the two of them, obviously trying to figure out how the silence came to be.

Motioning for him to rise with a sweeping movement of her free hand, Jane smiled softly at him.

"It'll be all right," she said in a hushed tone. "Just give me a few minutes alone with her, okay?"

She sat down in the rocking chair and cradled Joy in her arms. The baby sighed, her eyes locking onto Jane's face. The love that swelled in Jane's heart actually hurt. But the achy feeling was wonderful. She hadn't rocked Joy to sleep in a week…a week that somehow felt like many months.

Tearing her gaze from Joy's, Jane looked up at Greg, who still seemed in a daze. Without a word, he stared at the two of them for a second or two. Then he turned on a silent heel and stole from the room.

Later, after Joy had been sung to sleep and tucked snuggly into her crib, Jane found Greg sitting at the kitchen table, a mug of fragrant coffee hugged tight between his hands.

"Can I get you some?" he offered, indicating the coffee with a nod.

Jane shook her head. "I really shouldn't stay. I have to find a place to sleep tonight. I guess I'll go back to the hotel. I just hope they have a—"

"No," Greg interrupted. "Stay here. At least for tonight."

Something akin to giddy delight burst inside her like miniature fireworks. But she refused to allow her hopes to rise to too great a height.

He poured her a cup of coffee and set it down in front of the chair adjacent to the one in which he'd been sitting. Then he retrieved the sugar bowl, cream pitcher and a spoon from the counter and set them on the table.

"Sit down." And when she hesitated, he said, "Please."

So she sat.

"I just can't get over it. How good you are with her, I mean."

He laced the fingers of both hands around his mug again, and Jane got the distinct impression it was a habit of which he wasn't even aware.

Feeling a bit awkward, Jane quietly quipped, "I guess it's just a woman thing."

One corner of his mouth quirked. "Now, that's not very politically correct, is it?"

They shared a grin, a soft laugh, and the tenseness in him seemed to lessen.

"Besides," he continued, "it's not just that you're a woman. Joy cries often with Rachel, my office manager. She cries with the nurses in the office, too. But she just seems to be…I don't know…more *comfortable* with you than she is with anyone else." He stared into his mug, studying the steamy brown liquid. Murmuring almost to himself, he added, "Even her own mother."

Jane started, her spoon clanging against the side of the porcelain. His mention of Pricilla couldn't have been more perfect. Finding her sister, discovering how Joy came to be here in Greg's house was only a casual question away. All Jane had to do was ask about the obvious absence of Joy's mother.

But she remained silent. She couldn't afford to ask, actually. Greg was right in the middle of commending Jane on her care of Joy. On the easy relationship she'd established with his baby girl in what, to him, was an amazingly short time. Jane didn't want to ruin this moment by diverting his attention. Having the chance to remain here with Joy took precedence over everything else. Even finding Pricilla.

Suddenly, his intense green eyes were locked on her, reaching, digging, seeming to perceive everything about her. Jane grew nervous under his scrutiny.

Finally, he asked, "Why is that?"

She paused long enough to run her tongue over

her lips. Maybe she should have diverted his attention. Her shoulder lifted in a merest of shrugs. "Some people just…click. Maybe your daughter and I are soul mates."

Again, one corner of his mouth tipped up in the most sexy half grin Jane had ever seen.

"*Soul mates* is a term usually used to describe a special something between a woman and a man…not a woman and a child."

His voice was velvety, caressing, and the sound of it caused a shiver to cascade down her spine like a warm, tropical waterfall, and the small hairs at the back of her neck stood on end. Lord, but the man was attractive.

Silently, she warned herself not to let the conversation veer off its path. She leaned against the chair back. "You know, maternal instinct can be an awesome force." She smiled at him. Then she repeated, "*Awesome.* And some women have more than their fair share."

It was a belief on to which she'd always held fast. No matter what kind of miserable hand fate might have dealt her where motherhood was concerned.

He released his laced grip on the mug and reached up to worry his chin between his index finger and thumb. It was obvious to her that something was churning in his head.

Then he reached over and covered her hand with his palm, the warmth of his skin sending jolts of heat skittering up her arm, over every square inch of her skin. She wanted to pull away from him, knew she should, but she didn't.

"Listen," he said at last, "why don't you stay on?

We'll have two days to get to know each other. I'm not on call this weekend, so I don't have to be back into the office until Monday, unless there's an emergency. Tomorrow, you can call your previous employer and ask him to fax a reference to my office. And you can have your sister call me. I'd like to talk to her. About your experience taking care of her child.''

Jane felt elated. But something kept her from showing it.

"B-but what about your friends? What will they say? You made it clear that they disapprove of my being here looking after Joy."

She had to test him. See how determined he was to have her stay. She hated the idea of unpacking, of getting settled, only to be asked to leave again come morning after Greg's other doctor friends had a chance to talk to him.

"This is *my* life," he said. "And Joy is my daughter. Sometimes a man just has to put his foot down and do what he feels is right."

The relief that flooded through her made her feel dizzy with happiness.

"So, will you stay?"

Trying not to smile too brightly, Jane said, "Of course, I will."

She would not like him, damn it! She wouldn't allow herself to do such a thing.

Jane woke up feeling grumpy on Sunday morning with these very thoughts running through her head.

Saturday had been sunny. And although November had come in with the coldest temperatures Pennsylvania had seen in years, Greg and Jane had bundled Joy up and had driven to the nearest park to watch the ice skaters skim across the frozen, shallow pond. They had taken a brisk walk, pushing Joy in her stroller. And then they had stopped at a local eatery for some warm and spicy apple cider.

There had been times during the day when Jane was struck with the notion that this was how families were meant to be. Laughing and playing. Just being together. And each time she'd made this connection, she'd paused, unable to avoid making a comparison to her own and her sister's sorely lacking childhood.

Once, as she was pondering this vast contrast, Greg had begun to stare at her. Of course, he hadn't known what had been floating through her mind, but he had shown a surprisingly gentle concern about the sadness he'd evidently discerned in her eyes. Jane had simply smiled, waved away his apprehension and had run off to make a snow angel in the pitifully light dusting of snow. Joy didn't seem to mind the lack of the frozen stuff. She giggled delightedly as Jane lay on the ground and waved her arms and legs wildly to make the angel's wings and gown.

Greg had showered attention on his daughter all day long. And he'd been polite and pleasant to Jane, as well. He was nothing like the mean and nasty ogre Jane had imagined him to be. He never even came close to the selfish and petty man Pricilla had described so many times while she had been pregnant with Joy.

This behavior was confusing, Jane silently determined this Sunday morning as she kicked back the coverlet, swung her legs over the edge of the mattress and sat up. She combed her fingers though her tangled hair. But she knew he was not the good guy he was making himself out to be. And she refused to like him.

She knew his secrets. She knew he'd refused to give Pricilla money or help of any kind unless he was given full custody of his child. Jane knew this to be the truth. Any man who tried to blackmail the mother of his baby in this manner did not have a good heart.

No, he wasn't a good guy. He couldn't keep up the act forever. He would crack soon. Jane just knew he would. All she had to do was give him time. And everyone knew, to disreputable people, time was like a hefty length of rope. Give them enough of it and they would eventually hang themselves.

On her way out of the bathroom, she met Greg in the hallway. He'd obviously showered and dressed, the luscious scent of his woodsy cologne wafting in the air, and the sight of his handsome face had her feeling even more grumpy than before.

Why did her blood seem to heat up at the mere sight of him? Automatically, she reached up and clutched the facings of her satin bathrobe closer together, as if this action might somehow protect her from her body's instinctive and uncontrollable reactions to him.

Protection? The thought irritated her. She didn't need protection from the likes of him.

The protection you need is from yourself. The whispery words made her frown.

''Morning.'' His smile was like the brightest sunshine.

Her frown deepened into a scowl and she grunted an unintelligible greeting, trying to slip past him.

"Whoa, there." He reached out, snagging the sleeve of her thin dressing gown in his fingers.

Pausing, she cut her eyes up to him. She really wasn't in the mood. Not when she felt so darned confused by this man.

He chuckled, and Jane felt heat skitter in the pit of her belly. *Darn.* She hated feeling so out of control. This had never happened to her before. With anyone. Ever.

"Not a morning person, huh?" he asked, humor tinting his silky tone. "It's a good thing I've already brewed a pot of coffee. That should soothe the morning beast."

He was trying to make her smile. Make her laugh at herself. But she wouldn't give him the satisfaction. Not after awaking to such disturbing thoughts. "Thanks. I'll have a cup shortly. I'm going to get dressed first."

She made her way back to her room, sensing that he hadn't yet moved from where he stood in the hallway behind her. His gaze was like a tap on her shoulder.

When she reached her door, he called after her, "It's a good thing I perked the double-dynamite brand. The caffeine content is guaranteed to kill the beast. Says so right on the label." His brows rose, his sexy mouth widening in a grin as he added, "Or your money back."

A smile twisted her lips, despite her dark disposition. She sighed, reluctant to relinquish her hold on this gray mood. "I appreciate that," she told him.

"I'll be right there." Then she went into her room and closed the door.

Have you lost your mind? she silently railed at herself.

She couldn't afford to be unpleasant to Greg. The situation she was in was too tenuous for her to be snippy and sullen, no matter what she thought of his behavior toward Pricilla. Her job as Joy's nanny was still on the line, was still in its trial stages. She needed to be on her best behavior.

Ah, secrets. They were awful little pests. Irritants that caused a person headaches she didn't need. Burdens that caused a person to do things she wouldn't normally do. She had her secrets. And Greg had his. Well, at least he *thought* he had his.

The dreadful thing about secrets was that they could jump up and bite you on the butt if you weren't careful. So the question that ran through Jane's mind as she dressed was how to go about continuing to protect hers.

She had a letter of recommendation that needed materializing. Not to mention the telephone call from her sister that Greg was waiting for. How was she going to pull this off?

Yesterday, she'd been too busy with Greg and Joy in the park to even think about providing him with the things he'd requested. Evidently, he, too, had been too preoccupied to remember that her character needed vouching for. But the letter and the telephone call were weighing heavy on her mind now. And, heavens above, how she hated the idea of being forced to lie yet again. She was not a devious person. However, if she wanted to remain here with Joy, telling more lies was exactly what she was going to have to do.

Jane dressed quickly in jeans and a sweater. She slipped her feet into warm socks and leather loafers and gave her face a cursory glance in the mirror. The coating of mascara she'd given her lashes earlier in the bathroom made her blue-gray eyes stand out a bit more than usual.

She exhaled. She'd have to do. It wasn't that she thought she was ugly. But she sure didn't have the features of classic beauty. Like Pricilla.

Suddenly, she squared her shoulders, and straightened her spine as she gazed at her image. Consternation bit into her brow. She'd never focused on her looks before. So why was she so concerned with what she looked like now? Not even wanting to acknowledge the query, let alone try to come up with an answer to it, she shoved the thought from her mind, turned away from the mirror and headed out the door.

Silent words of warning echoed through her head. *Be nice*. If she wasn't, she just might find herself sitting out on the curb, missing Joy miserably. She didn't have to like the man. She just had to *be nice*.

She smelled the smoky scent of bacon in the air, heard the sizzling, before she entered the kitchen. Her stomach grumbled with gratitude.

"Wow," she remarked when she saw him standing by the stove. "Smells wonderful."

Glancing over at the empty high chair, she asked, "Joy's still sleeping?"

"Yes, but not for long, I'm sure." He focused on scooping the strips of bacon from the pan. "Why don't you start the toast while I scramble some eggs?''

"Sure."

After plunking slices of wheat bread into the toaster, Jane went to pour herself a cup of coffee. Leaning her hip against the counter, she took a sip and sighed. "Nectar of the gods."

He chuckled and she offered up a grin. If he could display his best manners, his charm-the-clouds-from-the-sky charisma, then so could she.

While he cooked the eggs, his attention riveted to the task, she took a moment to study him. His hair was the deepest red she'd ever seen. Bronzed mahogany. Glossy and thick with a slight wave, it was cut in a clean, traditional style. And he had nicely shaped ears. His jaw and neck were smooth, clean-shaven. His nose—

The toast popped up behind her and she started.

"Butter's on the table," he said softly.

Something in the quality of his tone gave her the distinct impression that Greg knew she'd been inspecting him. Ogling him, really. Jane felt blood rushing to her face, her skin flushing red hot. Moving first to the table to retrieve the butter, then to the toaster, she spent several moments too occupied with what should have been the simple task of buttering the toast. She didn't dare raise her eyes in his direction.

She didn't like the awkwardness that blossomed suddenly and abundantly like the sweet but cloying scent of too many hothouse flowers in a too-small space. The strain seemed to swell, to grow more intense with each passing second. It confused her. Was it all in her imagination? She'd never experienced this kind of uncomfortable tension before.

He divided the eggs between two plates, and without warning she was overwhelmed by anxiety at the idea of sitting alone at the table with him.

The quivery feeling in her belly got the best of her. "I'll go check on Joy."

"No, no," he told her. "Let's eat while we can. If I've learned one thing since my beautiful daughter's been with me it's that every free moment must be taken full advantage of."

Since his daughter had been with him. Humph. He made it sound as if he'd been raising his daughter for months rather than mere days.

He set the plates on the table, then reached for the platter of bacon. She carried the toast over and set it down.

"Orange juice?" he asked as he opened the door of the refrigerator.

She gave a quick nod of assent. Slowly, she pulled out the chair and lowered herself into it.

He leaned over her slightly as he poured the juice into her glass. The warm scent of him wafted around her, his now-familiar woodsy cologne enveloping her in something akin to a physical embrace. Unwittingly, her eyelids lowered and she inhaled, allowing herself a moment to bask in the heat of him, in the nearness of him. Never in a million years would she admit that she thought he smelled even better than frying bacon.

Her eyes popped open. Had she really just compared Greg's sensuous scent to that of crisp and delicious breakfast meat? It was a good thing he'd come out favorably in the comparison. Pressing her lips together, she successfully subdued the urge to giggle.

Giggle? The very idea offended her, insulted her intelligence. She'd never giggled in her life. Something strange was happening to her. She felt like some silly schoolgirl who was intent on making an impression on someone she felt attracted—

Is that what this giddiness she was feeling was all about? *Was she feeling attracted to Greg Hamilton?*

It was a ludicrous notion. An utterly ridiculous idea.

Yes, he was a handsome man with his deep, wavy red hair, his forest-green eyes, his delectable dimples, but surely—

She cast him a covert glance. Felt her pulse quicken, her skin grow prickly.

Lord, above! She *was* attracted to him.

Then yet another miserable thought rolled into her head: it had been so long since she'd felt attracted to any man that it had taken her two whole days of experiencing—suffering, really—these strange reactions before she realized what it was that was plaguing her. She stifled a groan.

Well, who could blame her for not dating? she silently wondered. She'd been busy raising her niece these past ten months. And before that, she'd been busy working to keep a roof over her pregnant sister's head. And before that—

"Pass the toast, please."

His request shook her out of her reverie. She held up the plate and he took a slice. He scooped up a forkful of eggs, slid the utensil between his lips. He chewed, his jaw tensing…*handsomely*.

Darn it, she would not allow some foolish physical attraction to rule her body. Or her mind. She could fight this. And she would.

What she needed was a distraction. And what better diversion than conversation? Conversation that verged on the dangerous side…dangerous enough to push this idiocy from her thoughts and keep her on her toes.

Before she had a chance to think, she dove right in. "If you don't mind my asking," she began, "what happened to Joy's mother?"

Immediately, she felt the need to show just how little she knew about the subject by adding, "Are you a widower? Divorced?"

He was a successful doctor. Respected. Trusted by his patients, his friends, his colleagues. He wouldn't dare admit to having a baby with a woman without going through the proper channel of getting married first. Surely, he would conjure a barrel full of lies. He'd fabricate his past, and in doing so, he'd lift the mask he wore, giving her a peek at his true colors. He'd be showing her his honest-to-goodness character without ever realizing he was doing it. And that's what she needed in order to banish this absurd attraction she was feeling.

"Actually," he said, "I've never been married."

Of their own volition, her brows rose in surprise when she heard him speak what must be the truth. Now the guilt she felt over her own lies swelled even more.

He chuckled, setting his fork down. "Don't look

so astonished. For every out-of-wedlock mother there is in the world, there's usually an out-of-wedlock father.''

Her voice was nowhere to be found. Finally, she croaked, ''That's true, I guess. But where is Joy's mother? And what about your parents? Sisters, brothers? You haven't had anyone to help you with Joy all these months?''

Her intent was to force him to reveal the circumstances surrounding how Joy came to be with him.

''I have no brothers or sisters, and my parents have been dead for several years. I came late in their lives, a bit unexpectedly.''

Jane's breath left her in a whispery apology. She'd had no idea he was all alone in the world, otherwise she wouldn't have been so brash.

''It's okay,'' he told her. ''I have Travis and Sloan. One of the things that bond the three of us is our lack of family support. So we support one another.''

The juice glass looked tiny in his grip. She noticed that the dark hairs on the back of his hand lay flat, and his skin was taut over bones, muscle and sinew. A vivid image of that hand smoothing over her bare shoulder assaulted her brain with crystal clarity, and she blinked.

Lifting the glass to his lips in what seemed to her to be slow motion, he drained it in just a few swallows and then placed it back on the table. The seconds ticked slowly by, and even though his unexpected answer about his family—or lack thereof—had taken some of the wind out of her sails, Jane still wanted to hear what he had to say about Joy's mother.

Finally, he leveled his intensely green eyes on her and said, "I'm not very proud of having to admit this, but before last Friday, I didn't even know I was a father."

Ah, so the lies were about to rain down. She chewed a bite of toast without being aware of its taste or texture on her tongue. It could have been a piece of corrugated cardboard for all she noticed.

"About eighteen months ago, I had a few dates with a woman," he continued, "I had a—a—"

"A *fling?*" Jane quickly provided, enjoying the word-jab as if it had been a swift uppercut with a well-placed fist to the jaw.

He instantly averted his eyes from hers, and Jane actually felt embarrassment emanating—no, *pulsing*—from him in waves.

He nodded, slowly. "Yeah."

He sighed, something that looked amazingly like regret making his broad shoulders sag. His gaze rose to hers once more, and his spine straightened. And Jane was sure from his posture, from the intensity in his eyes, that he wanted her to believe he was facing up to something. When he next spoke, his tone was barely more than a whisper.

"Yeah, I had a fling. A very brief affair that resulted in a pregnancy…and ultimately a child. My child. My baby girl."

Just then, Joy cried out for someone's attention. Jane automatically pushed back her chair, but Greg beat her to the punch.

"I'll go," he told her. "You finish eating." He

offered her a lopsided grin. "You're going to have to learn to eat faster."

Once she was alone, she noticed that Greg had cleaned his plate. And she? Well, she had eaten exactly one small bite of her now stone-cold toast.

Chapter Four

He was such a good liar!

Jane folded Joy's little pants and shirts as she pulled them out of the dryer. She was alone in Greg's spacious apartment. He'd taken Joy out to do the weekly grocery shopping and Jane had stayed behind to do some laundry and a little cleaning.

She'd suggested that, since it was afternoon and Joy would soon be needing a nap, he should leave Joy home with Jane. However, Greg had insisted on taking his daughter with him. She hadn't been able to blame him, really. Not while he was still feeling cautious about having hired her. And she hadn't yet provided the character references he'd requested.

Although it was grudgingly, Jane had to admire the way Greg seemed so protective of Joy. Jane didn't want to admire anything about the man, but he obviously cared about the baby—loved her. His paternal instinct seemed strong. Jane had to give the man that much, at least.

One of Greg's T-shirts must have gotten mixed up with Joy's clothes. Jane gave it a good shake, tucked the top of the shirt under her chin and hand-smoothed the wrinkles out of it, pressing it against her body. The shirt was still warm from the dryer. And the clean, heated smell of it made her fingertips tingle.

She had no trouble imagining the fabric stretching taut across Greg's back. Closing her eyes, she let her palm glide over the soft material, flattening it against her abdomen, letting her hand rise slowly, slowly, up and over her breasts. For an instant, it wasn't her hand at all, but his. His strong, virile touch. Burning with desire. For her.

Her nipples hardened into tiny, painful buds. Jane sucked in air in a gasp, her eyes opening wide.

Tossing the shirt onto the top of the dryer, she angrily murmured, "What is wrong with you?" She shook her head. "You've completely lost your mind, *that's* what's wrong with you."

She'd known this man exactly two days. She had no business whatsoever fantasizing about him.

You're not the kind of woman he'd ever be attracted to.

The thought made her lips press together tightly. Pricilla had been perfect for the wealthy, successful doctor. With her thick platinum mane, her big baby-blue eyes, Pricilla was the type of woman men such as Greg liked to have draped on their arms.

Pricilla was the rare queen bee, beautiful and pampered, while Jane was much more like a drone, the one who kept things organized and running, the one who was run-of-the-mill, the one who came a dime a dozen. Such a woman would never capture Greg's attention.

"That's good, because I don't *want* his attention," she muttered, snatching up a pair of tiny socks and rolling them together.

So why the erotic fantasies? She swatted at the question as if it were a stubborn buzzing bee intent on irritating her.

Even if she allowed herself to indulge in a little flight of fancy, Jane knew she would never have a chance with the man. She was in his house under false pretenses. She'd lied to him. Again and again. Purposefully. Deliberately. And he was bound to discover her true identity before too long.

Bound to? The silent question mocked her. There was really no doubt that he would discover her lies…because she was the one who was going to have to break down in the end and be totally honest.

He'll eventually find out who you really are, a voice in her mind intoned, *but he needn't discover all your secrets…secrets that keep you from having a relationship with* any *man.* The nightmarish thought made her shiver, and a gray dread seemed to fill her as it had since she'd learned the truth about herself, about her body. The memories of the rejections she'd ultimately received from the few men she'd grown close to chilled her.

Stop it, she silently commanded. No one needs to know. And to dwell on bad thoughts would only depress her even further.

She felt so bad for lying her way into Greg's

house. But it had been necessary. For her sanity. She had almost gone stark raving mad during the days Joy had been missing.

Besides, Greg had lied, too. Although, Jane did have enough sense to know that his lies didn't cancel out hers. Two wrongs were just that. Two wrongs.

Still, he lied so well, Jane thought. This morning when he'd revealed that he hadn't known he was a father before Pricilla and Joy had shown up on his doorstep a week ago, Jane had nearly gasped right out loud. He'd told the lie with a straight face. As if he really believed it. He'd lied with such…such *honesty,* that Jane had been left speechless.

Maybe, a tiny voice intoned from somewhere at the back of her brain, *maybe he was telling the truth.*

The idea shocked her. She walked away from the open dryer, paced down the hallway. Her steps led her unwittingly to her niece's bedroom, right up to the crib, and she smoothed her fingers back and forth across the rail as she stared unseeingly at the brightly colored mobile hanging over it.

Maybe Greg hadn't known about Joy.

No, Jane refused to believe that. If that were true, then oodles and oodles of questions would have to be raised regarding Pricilla's honesty. And Jane didn't want to think that her sister was *that* deceitful. That hurtful. Sure, Pricilla might sneak out of the house to go to this party or that one, but she would never look Jane in the eye and tell her bold-faced lies. Especially when it came to sorely needed money for Joy's living and medical expenses. Jane had worked so darned hard to make ends meet. Pricilla would never have— No, it had to be Greg who was being dishonest. He was lying. Jane was sure of it.

Greg arrived home with Joy, the baby's tears sending Jane running toward the front door.

"You were right." Greg sighed, his green eyes revealing his regret for not following Jane's advice. "She was ready for a nap and I'd only finished about half the grocery shopping. I tried to placate her, but—"

Jane scooped Joy from Greg's arms. "I'll go put her to bed."

He looked so exhausted, so grateful, and Jane smiled at him.

"I'll get the grocery bags from the car."

She nodded and headed off toward the baby's room, crooning sweet nothings into her niece's ear. After less than five minutes of rocking and softly sung lullabies, Joy was fast asleep. Jane just sat, enjoying the moment. This is what it must feel like to be a mother. A mommy. This warm and fuzzy love that turned a woman's heart all mushy and achy. There simply wasn't a more beautiful feeling to be experienced in all the universe.

Curling a lock of Joy's hair gently around her finger, Jane rocked and breathed in the sweet baby smell wafting in the air. She'd do anything to remain with her niece. Anything.

When Joy was tucked into bed, Jane went back into the kitchen to help Greg put away the groceries.

"The house looks great." He stood at the table taking boxes and cans from the plastic bags he'd carried in while she was putting Joy down for her nap.

"I didn't finish the laundry."

He chuckled, and Jane felt something grow all quivery in the pit of her belly at the rich, vibrating sound.

"I've learned that, with a baby in the house, laundry is something that never gets finished," he said.

She could only nod in agreement.

"I was able to reach my old boss," Jane told him. "He's going to fax a letter to your office today. It should be waiting for you when you arrive at work tomorrow."

"Great."

The begging and pleading it had taken to get Max to agree to write a letter of recommendation had about worn Jane to a frazzle. Max had demanded to know why he should do anything for her when she'd walked out on him like she had. Jane had had to remind him of all the times she'd come in to work on her days off when his other waitresses hadn't even bothered to call in sick, how she'd worked even when she was ill, how she'd worked holidays, how she'd filled in even when Max's kitchen help hadn't shown up.

In the end, he'd grudgingly agreed to write a letter stating she'd been a good employee up until she'd walked out for no good reason. He'd wanted to know what she was doing working for a doctor...what did she know about the medical field when all her experience had been in waiting tables, he'd accused. She'd successfully sidestepped his questions. She didn't want anyone to know what she was up to just yet. There were plenty of ways for her to mess up and reveal her true identity without giving anyone else the opportunity to do it. Not that she thought Max was that mean, but playing it safe was for the best for now.

"Did you speak with your sister?" Greg asked. "Did she agree to talk with me?"

Jane moistened her lips. "Well, I couldn't reach her. But that's not surprising. She's...always running here and there...working odd hours. I'll try her again later."

He put a pound of butter into the refrigerator. "The letter from your boss will satisfy me for the moment. But I would like to talk to your sister."

Her head bobbed silently and then she headed off to put the new tube of toothpaste and bottle of shampoo in the bathroom cabinet. Oh, heavens, how she hated lying. She was going to trip up and get her story all confused if she wasn't careful.

Now she'd have to remember she'd told him her sister worked a job that called for odd hours. When in reality, Pricilla didn't even have a job. What if Greg asked what kind of occupation her sister had?

Jane closed the bathroom cabinet and heaved a sigh. Lying wasn't for the faint of heart, that was for sure.

"Hey."

Greg's voice startled her nearly out of her skin, and she turned to see him standing in the bathroom doorway.

He grinned. "Didn't mean to scare you. What's got you so on edge?" Before she could respond, he said, "Here. Catch. This goes under the sink."

He tossed a package of toilet tissue into the air. She caught it easily and stored it away.

What had her so on edge? he'd asked. When she faced him once more with every intention of responding to his query, she saw that he had evidently gone back to the kitchen. She looked at her face in the mirror. The answer was easy. Murderers, thieves and liars led a paranoid existence. Especially murderers, thieves and liars who had been blessed—or cursed, as the case may be—with a healthy conscience.

Okay, maybe lumping herself in with murderers and thieves was being a bit overly dramatic. But she sure was feeling awfully paranoid. And guilty as sin.

Back in the kitchen, Greg was just putting the fresh produce away. She saw the table laden with jars of baby food, pureed apples and pears, green beans and peas, boxes of rice cereal and zwieback biscuits, cans of formula, packages of diapers. The thought of him shopping up and down the baby aisle in the grocery store for all the things Joy would need through the week…well, Jane found the idea quite endearing.

"Wow," she whispered. "You didn't forget a thing."

"You think so?"

There was clear uncertainty in his question, and Jane found that charming, too. He wanted to be a good parent, to provide Joy with everything she would need. He came to stand beside her and looked down at his purchases.

"I was worried. I had to go out about a million times last week. First for diapers, then for baby formula and again when we ran out of cereal. I was trying to avoid doing that this week, if it's at all possible.'' He chuckled as he picked up a squeaky toy he'd bought. ''I couldn't resist this.'' He pressed the colorful wheel-shaped teether. ''I thought about getting it out to distract her in the car, but I knew she was too upset for that. So I just hurried home as fast as I could. What she needed was a nap. Not a new toy.''

Instincts. He had a daddy's instincts. Heat curled low in her gut, and Jane realized she found the idea to be…*sexy*. Startlingly so. It was silly, really. But she couldn't help herself.

His tone was soft as he said, ''You know, when you smile like that, those blue-gray eyes of yours twinkle like stars in a clear night sky.''

She blinked. Blue-gray? Twinkle? Like stars in the sky? She'd never heard herself described in such a manner. She'd always thought her eyes were a dreary gray. Like an overcast day. But here Greg was comparing her gaze to glittering stars. Her smile broadened of its own accord.

''Thanks,'' she whispered, unable to keep her chin from dipping, her eyes from cutting up at him through lowered lashes. She felt suddenly shy. Bashful.

For a moment, they stood there, just smiling at each other. Jane basking in his compliment, and he…well, she had no clue what he might be thinking.

At last he said, ''We never got a chance to finish our conversation this morning.''

''Our conversation?'' For a split second she felt at a complete loss. His unexpected flattery had really thrown her for a loop. As if she were on some wild amusement park ride.

"About Pricilla," he continued, carrying several jars of the baby food to the pantry. "Joy's mother."

"Oh, yes. Of course." At the mention of her sister's name, Jane's heart seemed to sink right down to her ankles. "Joy's mother. I asked you where she was this morning."

He nodded, coming back for a second haul of the tiny jars. She watched his big hands span across the jar lids, and she couldn't help but remember how his touch had been so gentle on Friday when he'd listened to the sound of her heart. Blood whooshed through her ears at the memory.

Focus, darn you!

"Well, like I said—" his back was to her as he put away the fruit and vegetables "—I didn't know Pricilla and I were parents until she showed up on my doorstep last week. She just knocked on the door, told me I was a dad and then proceeded to drop off Joy and all her belongings."

An uneasy feeling crept over Jane.

"Just like that?" she asked him. "She just showed up and handed over the baby?"

"Just like that." He came back to the table for the boxes of cereal and teething biscuits. "She gave very little explanation. Only that she'd tried to raise Joy and just couldn't do it. She did look terribly harried. And Joy was crying her little eyes out when they arrived. Hungry. Tired. She was a handful for quite a while before I got her calmed down."

He's lying. He's lying. Jane kept chanting the silent words. Pricilla wouldn't do such a thing. She wouldn't just dump off her daughter as Greg was describing.

The awful memory of arriving home before her sister...of catching Pricilla carrying Joy across the lawn, coming from the neighbor's, and the baby with no coat to ward off the chilly fall wind. Jane grasped the back of the kitchen chair. Maybe Pricilla would leave her daughter with a sitter for an evening, but surely she'd never unload Joy for good. Never. Greg was lying. Yet, uneasiness crawled around in her chest like a thousand creepy little spiders.

"Pricilla didn't stay long," he continued. "She handed me Joy's birth certificate. I was named her daddy right there on the dotted line. But then, I realized Joy was mine as soon as I got a chance to really look at her. She's my very image, don't you think? Right down to the dimples."

Jane knew she should be pitching in, helping Greg put the baby food into the pantry. But she was too overwhelmed by what she was hearing to move, to think clearly, to speak, so she simply stood there holding on to the chair back for dear life.

"Oh, and she gave me what few medical records she had, too. Thank goodness she'd started Joy on her baby shots. And she kept good records of them, too. For that, I'm thankful."

Again his back was turned to her as he faced the pantry. Joy's birth certificate and inoculation record booklet. Jane hadn't thought to check to see if they were still in the file cabinet at home. The dread in her belly thickened to what felt like cement.

"Pricilla told me not to call her." This time his chuckle was without humor and came out sounding more like a disdainful sneer. "Said she'd call me, if and when she ever wanted to see Joy again." He came to stand by the table next to her and, heaved a sigh. "I've been thinking about seeing a lawyer. I'd like to have permanent custody of my baby girl."

Somehow, Jane got through the rest of the afternoon. Thankfully, Joy had only slept an hour and then the child was refreshed and ready to be occupied. Jane was happy to oblige. Playing with the baby had given her something to do with her hands, something on which to focus her thoughts. She hadn't wanted to think about Pricilla. And she hadn't wanted to wonder one more second if Greg had been telling the truth. She hadn't been up to working it all out. Not then. She just hadn't.

But now in the wee hours of Monday morning when all she'd done was toss and turn and then toss some more, she couldn't help but think about this situation. Her sister. Greg. Joy. The deceitful predicament she now found herself in. Guilt ran through her mind like a wild, uncontrollable brushfire searing to ash all her positive explanations, all her logical motivations, as if they were bone-dry tinder.

The whole time Greg had been telling her his side of how Joy came to be living with him, the overwhelming dread inside Jane had grown and swelled. He was being truthful. She wanted to believe he was lying, but the honesty shining in his clear forest-green eyes—in his handsome face—was unmistakable. Heck, her own intuition had been confirmation enough. His body language had been easy and open.

Nothing at all what she'd have expected from a man who was fabricating a fantastic story.

Besides, what would have motivated him to lie to her? He didn't know who she was. He didn't know she had any ties to his child other than acting as Joy's nanny.

Sure, he might have wanted to make himself out as the one who had been wronged rather than looking like a bad guy, but he'd actually seemed regretful that he hadn't known about Joy until last week. And now it seemed he was going to see a lawyer about garnering custody. That act didn't fit with someone who had a cavalier attitude about parenthood. And neither did the tender and caring behavior Jane had seen Greg exhibit toward Joy. The man cherished his daughter. He loved her. Deeply. That much was evident.

All these facts left her a slim hand from which to draw conclusions, she realized as dread churned like dark, slimy waters in her gut. And every single conclusion had an extremely narrow focus: Pricilla.

Her body rigid with tension as she lay there in the dark, Jane realized she had been lied to. Not by Greg, but by Pricilla. Her sister. Her own flesh and blood.

For months and months during Pricilla's pregnancy, Jane had worked like a madwoman in the restaurant, taking on all the extra hours she could get from the other waitresses just so her sister could take it easy, take care of herself and the new baby growing inside her. Pricilla had always been a high-strung young woman, and during her pregnancy she'd needed a great deal of counsel, which Jane had provided as best she could in her role of big sister.

And once Joy had arrived, Jane had continued to work extra hours in order to give her sister time to heal, time to bond with her baby. However, the bonding never did seem to take place. And after recuperating a month or so, Pricilla had been determined to go back to her party life. Jane tried hard to be patient with her sister. As long as they watched their pennies, and Pricilla was there to watch Joy while Jane worked, the three of them survived fairly well on Jane's salary.

Yes, they had survived. But there had been so many things they had all done without…well, at least Jane and Joy had done without. Pricilla always seemed to find some man or other to take her to dinner or buy her an expensive haircut or tanning session or whatever other frivolity she thought she had to have.

To think that Joy had gone months without a high chair and a baby swing and all those other wonderful contraptions meant to make life simpler for parents. But those were luxuries Jane's budget simply couldn't afford. However, if Pricilla had gone to Greg, maybe Joy wouldn't have had to do without for so darned long.

Oh, Pricilla had *said* she'd gone to Greg. She said that Greg wanted absolutely nothing to do with the baby unless he could have the child, lock, stock and barrel. Jane's head had been filled with awful stories about the baby's father—stories she was now discovering were all lies.

The state would force the baby's father to pay support, Jane had told her sister, and she'd urged Pricilla to see someone at Social Services. But Pricilla always had some excuse or other about why she hadn't gone. Jane had finally come to the conclusion that Greg Hamilton was such a tyrant that Pricilla had been too afraid to face him in court.

Now Jane couldn't help but realize that Pricilla had lied about everything. She'd never gone to Greg for help. She'd never even told him he was going to be a father.

Why?

It hurt Jane terribly to think how hard she'd worked to keep a roof over Pricilla's head, food in her and her baby's stomachs, clothes on her child's back.

Oh, Jane didn't regret her efforts. Not one bit. She loved her family—with all her heart and soul. She'd have worked her fingers to the bone to provide for Joy. But her feelings had been battered and bruised by Pricilla for so long…ever since her sister had announced her pregnancy. And Jane hadn't even known the beating—in the guise of deceit—was going on.

Now she knew. And her heart ached with the knowledge. Her stomach filled with a lump of emotion, and that burning emotion slowly rose to fill her throat, burn her eyes with scalding tears.

The first sob that escaped her lips had been silent, and Jane snatched at the box of tissues on her nightstand, covering her mouth with one. But the more her brain churned over Pricilla's lies, the more she thought of how her sister had allowed her to work so hard, how she'd received little-to-no help with the bills or keeping the house…it was all too much.

Before she could stop them, tears were flowing

freely, her heart broken in what felt like a million razor-sharp shards that sliced and gouged her. Her breathing came in racking heaves. She tried hard to stay quiet, but the depth of her anguish was more than she could bear.

How? How could Pricilla just pack up and leave? How, after all Jane had done, could her sister just take Joy away with no word of where she had gone or when she had planned to come back?

Because she hadn't planned to return.

The whispery thought caused a shock wave of pain and desolation to roll through her, chilling her to the very marrow in her bones. A low moan surged from deep in her throat, as unstoppable as a tremulant earthquake.

Clutching the pillow to her chest, she tried in vain to squelch the agony that ripped at her heart. Why? *Why?* Why would her sister want to hurt her so badly? Why would she disappear with Joy when Jane did nothing but work hard to keep their small family together? Hot tears burned her cheeks. It just didn't make sense.

The soft knock on the bedroom door startled a gasp from her and she unwittingly pushed herself into a sitting position, stiff and straight, on the mattress.

"Jane?"

Greg's voice was gentle, questioning.

"Jane, it's me," he said. "Are you okay?"

When she didn't answer, he continued, "Can I come in?"

"No!" Blindly, she reached for more tissues,

hauling in deep breaths in an attempt to get herself under control. "I'm okay. I'm fine."

The last thing she wanted was for Greg to see her in this state. He'd expect an explanation, and she simply wasn't up to concocting any more lies. She felt bad enough as it was, having swallowed as truth all the bad things about him that Pricilla had fed her over the months.

Swiping the wad of tissues under her eyes and nose, Jane peered through the moonlight. Oh, how she wished she'd thought to lock the door before she'd gone to bed.

"But—"

She heard his hesitation, obvious concern turning his tone warm and low. The murmuring resonance of his voice made her muscles go weak and liquid. The feeling was surprising...and pleasant. In her everyday life, *she* was the one who usually did the worrying about others.

"—I heard you crying. Please. Let me come in."

The unexpected pleasure vanished in a flash when she saw the doorknob turning. Instantly, her eyes widened, her shoulders froze as rigid as steel, her limbs stiffened as she started through the darkness at the door.

He was coming in.

Chapter Five

Her first thought was to bury her head in the covers. At least then he wouldn't see her blotchy, tear-streaked face. She didn't need to turn on the light or stand in front of a mirror to know she looked a wreck.

The door inched open, and Greg's head and upper body appeared. Moonlight from the window gleamed on his mahogany hair. The darkness kept her from actually detecting the green of his eyes, but she did see the deep concern biting into his brow.

"You're not sick, are you?" he asked softly.

"No. I'm not sick."

Her inhalation was shaky. Desperate to control her emotions, she grasped the cotton blanket in her fists and held on tight. No matter how hurt she felt, she must not allow her torment to show in front of him. If she did, if she yielded to the tears burning the backs of her eyelids, if she accepted any consolation from him, the whole truth about her, about how and why she came to be in his home, would surely come tumbling from her lips. She just knew it. Yes, it was true that she'd figured out some things about Greg tonight—that he'd been just as wronged by Pricilla as she herself had been—however, Jane still didn't know this man well enough to gauge how he would react to the lies she'd told him. She had to protect herself. She had to protect her place here with Joy.

Smile. Make him believe you're okay. Even if you're not. And above all, don't cry. You must keep your wits about you.

"Tell me what's wrong. What has you so upset?"

Her heart melted at his whisper-soft request. He looked worried. And she took an odd comfort in the fact that his concern was focused directly on her.

"Did you have a bad dream?"

It never even entered her head to latch onto this excuse. She'd have loved to explain away her tears so easily, but he didn't deserve to hear any more lies. She might feel unable to reveal the truth just yet, but she didn't have to invent any more stories, either. This scheme of hers was complicated enough.

Jane shook her head in a silent, negative answer.

He approached the bed, coming close enough that she could smell the luscious woodsy scent of him, see the way his T-shirt pulled taut and sexy across his broad chest. Lord, why did her body betray her every single time she was in his presence?

"Honey," he began, but then he paused.

After a moment of evident indecision, he eased himself down on the very edge of the mattress beside her.

"You've helped me so much with Joy," he said, "and with the house. Please let me help you now. Talk to me."

The sincerity in his voice was her undoing. Over the past couple of days, this man had shown her that he was nothing but genuine. He was kind. Considerate. Caring. He'd taken her in when he thought she was homeless and unemployed.

And how had she returned his kindness? With nothing but lies.

Her resolve to keep silent about herself, about her secret, faltered. A strong urge to do the right thing rose up inside her, bright and flaring like a matchstick struck in the blackest night. Maybe he wouldn't toss her out on her ear if he learned the truth. Maybe…just maybe he would understand. Maybe she could explain the circumstances in a way that would even garner his sympathy.

But, she wondered frantically, where should she begin?

The recommendation. The reference from her sister. The call that wasn't going to come.

"Greg," she murmured, "there's something you need to know."

Another thing she'd learned about him this past weekend was that his occupation made him an excellent listener. He trained his silent gaze on her, waiting with what seemed the utmost patience.

"You see—" her words came haltingly "—my sister isn't going to call." Jane swallowed around the lump of fear that suddenly rose in her throat. Was she doing the right thing? In a rush, she continued,

"She's gone. I don't know where she is. Or when she'll be back. I need to tell you that I'm—"

"Oh, honey."

He pulled her to him; the feel of his muscular chest, hard and warm against her cheek, made her thoughts turn to utter chaos. Her brain went haywire as she found herself enveloped in his strong, protective arms.

"You're crying because you thought I'd fire you without a character reference from your sister?"

His soft chuckle reverberated against her cheekbone. Jane helplessly closed her eyes, enjoying the feel of him, the sound of him. Her heart kicked against her ribs with such force she was sure he must feel the pounding of it. Blood whooshed thickly through her ears.

With one side of her forehead pressed against the base of his throat, her ear flattened against his chest, she could feel the rise and fall of his breathing, hear the distinct thump of his heart. Why had he reached out for her? Why had he hugged her to him? She couldn't think clearly. She couldn't think at all!

Pushing himself a few inches away from her, he leveled his green eyes on hers.

"I want you to stop worrying. Do you hear me? I want you to dry your eyes and stop agonizing about this."

All she was able to do was study his gaze. Words wouldn't come. Neither would movement of any kind. She felt frozen in time. Like a wild, defenseless animal caught in the crosshairs of the scope of a gun.

She knew he meant his smile to be comforting. However, she found it dazzling—and terribly sensuous. And rather than calming her, it only served to further confuse her thinking processes, further stir her body's physical reactions to him.

"The call was just a formality," he said. "Tomorrow I'll have the letter from your former boss, right?"

He didn't seem to notice that she made no response whatsoever.

"And I've seen for myself how good you are with my little girl. The two of you have developed quite a relationship in a very short time. It's been—" his head shook back and forth the tiniest fraction "—remarkable."

Tell him. Tell him the truth!

But she couldn't. Not because she didn't want to. Not because she meant to continue to hide her true identity from him. It was just…he was so close. Too close. She felt lost. Lost in those forest-green eyes. Lost in the kindness he was showing her. Lost in the concern he was showing her. Lost in the heated touch of his hands on her upper arms. Lost in the warm and seductive scent of him, in his tenderness.

"You can stay," he told her. "I *want* you to stay. I'm sure I'll talk to your sister sometime." His tone softened even further as he added, "It's not important. I feel I know you. I think you're good for Joy. You'll stay, won't you? You do want to stay?"

Jane blinked. That was all she was able to do.

He was so good-hearted. And too damned handsome! Again she swallowed. But the lump of fear had dissolved only to be replaced with…something new. Something strange. Then she realized her throat burned. It burned with raw desire.

This was crazy! She needed to scoot away from him. She needed some distance. But she didn't move. Couldn't move. The hunger inside her grew with each passing millisecond.

She must break this mesmerizing spell she was under. *Speak,* her brain commanded. *Speak!* Mustering every ounce of her strength, she hoarsely whispered, "Thank you."

Why on earth was she expressing gratitude? The question he'd asked required a simple yes or no answer. He was going to think she was a lunatic. She *was* a lunatic.

His touch was feather soft as he slid his fingertips along the length of her jaw. His gaze intensified with some unnamable emotion. The air grew heavy. Throbbing.

"I'm the one who should be thanking you."

His tone was deliciously soft and enticing. The tension magnified. And all the oxygen in the room seemed to dissipate.

Then he did the most extraordinary thing. He inched toward her, closer and closer, and he covered her mouth with his.

His kiss was excruciatingly sweet and gentle. Just like his concern for her had been only moments before. Her heart felt squeezed with the preciousness of it. Of him.

Before she even had time to close her eyes, he'd pulled away from her, leaving her lips feeling cool and desolate and wanting more. Jane knew the uncertainty she felt had her eyes wide and staring. She tucked her bottom lip between her teeth, tasting the honeyed remnants of their sinfully soft kiss.

One corner of his mouth quirked upward.

"I should probably apologize for that," he whispered. Then his grin widened. "But I can't." He stood up, went to the door and then turned to face her. "You're a special woman. And I'm glad you're here. Now try to get some sleep. You're going to have a full day with Joy tomorrow. All on your own. You need your rest."

He opened the door, offering her one last smile. "Good night."

Jane sat there, alone in the dark, wondering what the heck had just happened between them and knowing that rest would be the last thing she'd be getting tonight.

"Well, to *me*—" Greg pointed at his own chest, leaning forward for emphasis "—this letter of recommendation sounds like it's coming from a disgruntled boss."

He sat at the large oak table in the conference room with Travis and Sloan. His friends had been surprised when he'd told them he'd allowed Jane to stay the weekend, and that the woman was with Joy now.

"Her former boss," Sloan said, "this Max, does say that Jane did a good job while she worked for him." He paused, looking over the fax that had been waiting for Greg when he arrived at work this morning. Then Sloan said, "However, it doesn't say why she left his employ."

"The important point is that *she* left the job," Greg asserted. "She wasn't fired. She was reliable. She was hardworking. She was responsible." He ticked off all the attributes the letter mentioned. "And up until she left the restaurant, she was an exceptional employee."

"But why did she leave?" Travis's inquiry made everyone go quiet for a moment. "And why didn't she give the customary two weeks' notice? I'd have to say that's a strike against her."

"Maybe." Tamping down a sudden mild irritation, Greg realized he shouldn't be annoyed at his friend and partner simply because he'd voiced a question. A very logical one at that. However, for some ungodly reason, Greg just didn't want his friends to find fault with Jane. He wanted her for his daughter's nanny. There was just something about her—something he couldn't quite put his finger on— that told him she deserved this job, that she'd do well in it, and that she wouldn't let him down.

"But," Greg continued, "what if she left her last job abruptly because of her boss? Because of this Max person?" He didn't quite know where he was taking this. He was speaking as quickly as the thoughts formed in his head. "What if this Max was harassing her? What if he was hitting on her? Asking her out on a date? And rather than take the pressure of working in that kind of environment, she quit."

Now it was Travis's turn to say, "Maybe."

Sloan softly, but firmly added, "Maybe not."

"Look," Greg said, "I spent the entire weekend with Jane. She's great with Joy. I couldn't ask for a more loving, nurturing person to be with my daughter while I'm at work." His brows shot upward. "And I *am* at work, I want you to notice. Early. This is the first morning meeting I've made since Joy came to live with me."

The expressions of the other two men relaxed in acknowledgment.

"Besides that—" Greg rushed to shoot home a final point before they had time to reload their bows with more arrows of criticism "—there are more recommendations coming. I expect a call from Jane's sister any time. Apparently, Jane practically raised her sister's baby."

Thinking it best to change the whole subject, Greg glanced down at the agenda that Rachel, their office manager, had typed up for the meeting.

"What's this listed here?" Greg asked Travis. "You need character references yourself?"

Greg thought this would be a great time to razz his friend a little, but the strain that tensed Travis's mouth killed his teasing comments before they even formed on his tongue.

"The Indian Council is asking for references now." Travis absently rubbed at his forehead with his fingertips. "They keep finding new reasons why I shouldn't adopt the boys."

Travis, half Kolheek Indian himself, had been trying for months to adopt a set of Kolheek twins. Several years earlier, he'd been instrumental in seeing that the children received a life-saving heart operation. The boys were now nearing the age where their chances of finding a good home were growing slimmer with each passing week. So Travis had taken it into his head to become the boys' father.

"I'll be happy to write you a glowing character reference," Sloan said.

"Me, too," Greg added. "I'll get right to work on it. I just don't understand what this Council of Elders could have against you."

It was hard to fathom that neither the state nor the federal government had any say in who adopted the children. On the Kolheek reservation, the council had the final say in who could or could not become parents of those orphaned twins.

"Well, I'm single," Travis said. "And that, I think, is the biggest part of the problem."

Greg chuckled, hoping to lighten his friend's dark mood. "You could always get married. Haven't you ever heard of a marriage of convenience?"

"I'm never getting married. You know that." Travis fairly growled the words. "I can raise Jared and Josh on my own. All I need to prove it is a chance. Look at Sloan. He's raising three girls. Three. And, you, too, Greg. You're doing okay as a single dad, aren't you?"

Holding his breath, Greg just smiled and hoped his friend's question was a rhetorical one. He hadn't been doing so hot at all as a single parent…until Jane had shown up to help smooth out the wrinkles of living with a ten-month-old baby.

The thought of Jane, and how she seemed to love his daughter, made him grow all warm inside. Who was he kidding? Yes, he was happy that Jane took good care of Joy, but what had him so churned up was that utterly delectable kiss he'd given her last night. He couldn't say what had possessed him to do such a thing. But he refused to feel badly about it.

"I'll make the council see that I can do it."

Travis's voice brought Greg abruptly back to the present.

"I *can* do it," Travis said, his tone emphatic.

"I know you can." Sloan was quick to agree.

"Sure, you can," Greg told his friend. "There's no doubt in my mind that you'll be a good father to those boys. Having a parent—even one who happens to be single—has to be better for the boys than living in an orphanage."

Travis's glance expressed a sudden uncertainty. "So, you guys don't mind helping me? You'll write something up and mail it to the reservation in Vermont?"

"Of course, we will," Sloan said automatically.

Greg didn't like seeing Travis so worried. "That's what friends are for, Travis. To pitch in when the chips are down."

"Thanks," Travis murmured.

But Greg didn't know how much good his reassurance did for his friend. It was pretty obvious that Travis wouldn't stop worrying until Jared and Josh were settled at home here in Philadelphia.

"You're welcome, buddy." Sloan stood up, reached over and patted Travis on the shoulder. "Like Greg said, this is what friends are for." Sloan then directed his gaze to Greg. "And I do have to say, I really am glad you attended today's meeting. We were going to talk about Thanksgiving dinner since it'll be here in a few weeks, before we all know it, actually. And if you weren't here, we were going to volunteer your apartment as the place for the celebration."

"I'll have dinner," Greg said, thinking the idea a

very good one. "I'll be happy to. It'll give you guys a chance to see Jane up close and personal." He smiled. "I think you'll like her."

Although he couldn't quite figure out why, he hoped his friends liked Jane as much as he did.

One week passed. And then another. And Jane was sure she had found nirvana. This is what it must feel like to be a stay-at-home mom. She enjoyed all the pleasures involved with raising her gorgeous baby Joy and none of the tiresome hassles of having to go out to work every evening as she had for the first ten months of her niece's life.

Jane could not fathom how she'd lived under the kind of stress she had for the last ten months: working in the restaurant every night until the wee hours of the morning, and then with only a few hours' sleep, getting up to tend Joy and clean the house so that Pricilla could sleep in or run off for the day with friends.

Love for Joy is what had fueled her energy through the stressful weeks, Jane surmised. She paused, knowing she had to admit that there was other fuel, too.

Guilt. She'd been plagued with tons of it all during Pricilla's pregnancy, and even more so after Joy was born. Jane felt terrible about the things she'd said to her sister in order to get Pricilla to carry the baby to term, the way she'd acted—

Jane pushed the thought from her mind. She'd only wanted what was best for Joy. If she hadn't behaved in that ugly manner—

Again, Jane did her damnedest to shove the idea

aside. Tears welled and scalded the backs of her eyelids just *thinking* about what might have been if Pricilla had had her way.

Mercifully, Joy's coos and giggles captured Jane's
attention.

"Hey, baby girl," she said softly, "how about if
we bundle up and go out for a walk?"

Jane believed Joy must be the smartest child on
earth. At ten-and-a-half-months old, the baby actually seemed to understand the word *walk* for, at the
sound of it, she dropped the rattle she'd been playing
with and reached outstretched arms toward Jane.

Changing Joy into a dry diaper would be the first
order of business, she thought, carrying her niece
toward the back of the apartment. When she passed
the door of Greg's room, the lingering scent of his
cologne had her steps slowing.

Ever since Greg had surprised her with that excruciatingly sweet kiss the first weekend she'd
moved in, something had happened. A startling
awareness had developed between them. An awareness that compressed the oxygen in the air whenever
they were together. An awareness that kept her feeling giddy all the time. It was ridiculous, really.

Of course, she could understand her own feelings.
He was a handsome man. It was only natural that
she'd find him appealing. His allure was more than
mere good looks. He was smart. And strong, physically and emotionally. He was the kind of man a
woman could lean on. And he was funny, too. He
made her laugh. He made her feel…good. But for
the life of her, she couldn't understand what he'd
ever see in her. Compared to Pricilla—and probably

every other woman Greg had ever dated—Jane was downright plain. Plain and undesirable.

However, she had to admit that this attraction, this awareness she felt throbbing between them, made her feel…pretty. When Greg looked at her with those gorgeous clear green eyes of his, when his intense gaze was leveled on her and was sparked with that mysterious interest, she could easily imagine herself as beautiful as a fashion model.

"Ha! Fat chance." Jane's bark of laughter was humorless and so loud it made Joy start. "I'm sorry, baby," she crooned as she fastened the diaper over her niece's bottom.

"Even if your daddy *was* interested in me," she said to Joy, "I'd be an idiot to think anything could ever come of it. As soon as he discovers my lies…and I've got to tell him, don't I, sweetie pie?—" she gave Joy a kiss on the forehead "—he's going to kick me out on my ear."

Guilt. It swelled in her chest until she felt water-logged. But she'd carried the emotion around for so long, first due to her behavior toward Pricilla and now due to the lies she'd told Greg, that the heavy emotion was starting to feel almost normal.

"Heaven forbid," she muttered. She tucked Joy's knit top into her corduroy trousers and smiled down at her niece. "Okay, let's go for that walk, my little honey bun."

Buttoning up Joy's coat and tucking the baby's curls under a warm hat, Jane couldn't wait to get out into the sunny but chilly November day. Maybe the brisk late fall breeze would clear her mind.

Jane said a quick hello to the doorman at the main

entrance of the apartment complex and then paused to put on Joy's mittens.

"If you don't mind my saying so, ma'am—"

The doorman's voice had Jane glancing up at him from where she leaned over the stroller.

"—your arrival surely has changed Dr. Greg." The man's mouth quirked up at one corner in a grin.

Curiosity planted itself between her brows in the form of a frown. "Oh?" She wondered what he could mean by the statement.

"Before you moved in with the baby," the doorman continued, "I was certain the complex administrator was going to replace Dr. Greg's front door with one that—" again, he smiled "—*revolved*. He sure was a lady-killer, that one. I don't mind tellin' ya, I was envious. Forced to live vicariously, opening the door for all those lovely ladies coming and going. But it looks like you tamed him. You and your little girl, that is."

Jane was stunned silent. If she was correctly understanding the man, he'd evidently mistaken her for Greg's live-in lover.

There was nothing vulgar or suggestive in the doorman's remarks. His smile was open and friendly. And Jane got the impression he simply meant to pay Greg—and her, for that matter—some sort of backhanded compliment. Although, for the life of her, she couldn't work up any appreciation. In fact, what she felt was angry and insulted.

"Let me set you straight on a few things." She straightened her spine and plunked her hand on her hip. "I have not *tamed* Dr. Greg, or anyone else for that matter." She felt her face flush hot. "I am not this baby's mother. I'm merely her nanny. And if this complex administrator you just spoke of were to get wind of your gossiping about the building's tenants, I'm sure your job just might be in grave jeopardy."

The doorman looked flabbergasted, to say the least. He blubbered, "B-but I was only...I didn't think—"

"*That* much is quite obvious."

"B-but," he stammered again. "I *like* Dr. Greg. I didn't mean any harm."

"I realize that. And that's the only reason I'm willing to keep this little incident between you and me. But I'd advise that, in the future, you keep your comments about the tenants to yourself. You *do* like your job, don't you?"

"Yes, ma'am," he said in a rush. "I'm awfully sorry, ma'am. I was only meaning to let you know that he must think an awful lot of you. I haven't seen him go out with a woman...other than you...in several weeks. And that's like some kind of record for Doc..."

His words trailed off as Jane placed her index finger against her lips in a gesture meant to make him stop talking.

Then he said, "I didn't know you were...just the nanny...."

Her eyes widened in exasperation when he didn't heed her silent warning. "Shh," Jane warned, her ire stirring yet again.

"My explanations—" the doorman looked miserable "—are only making it worse."

She nodded.

"I'm sorry," he said. "Really."

Jane simply sighed in anger and frustration, turned the stroller onto the sidewalk and started off down the street.

"Just the nanny." The words came out in a disgusted mutter.

In all honesty, she should thank the doorman. She needed to remember that "just the nanny" was all she was. And that's all she would ever be. The thoughts she'd been dwelling on since their kiss—that he was attracted to her, that he made her feel as pretty as Liz Taylor, that the two of them could ever have any kind of relationship—were lunacy. Total lunacy! For as soon as Greg discovered the truth about her—the truth about how she'd lied and manipulated her way into his home—he'd be as mad as a wet hen. And he'd never forgive her in a million years.

FREE BOOKS! FREE GIFT!

PLAY BANGO!

AND CLAIM 2 FREE BOOKS AND A FREE GIFT!

★ No Cost!
★ No Obligation to Buy!
★ No Purchase Necessary!

TURN THE PAGE TO PLAY

PLAY BANGO! AND GET THREE FREE GIFTS!

It looks like **BINGO**, it plays like **BINGO** but it's **FREE!**
HOW TO PLAY:

1. With a coin, scratch the Caller Card to reveal your 5 lucky numbers and see that they match your Bango Card. Then check the claim chart to discover what we have for you — 2 FREE BOOKS and a FREE GIFT — ALL YOURS, ALL FREE!

2. Send back the Bango card and you'll receive two brand-new Silhouette Romance® novels. These books have a cover price of $3.50 each in the U.S. and $3.99 each in Canada, but they are yours to keep absolutely free.

3. There's no catch. You're under no obligation to buy anything. We charge nothing — ZERO — for your first shipment. And you don't have to make any minimum number of purchases — not even one!

4. The fact is, thousands of readers enjoy receiving our books by mail from the Silhouette Reader Service™. They enjoy the convenience of home delivery…they like getting the best new novels at discount prices, BEFORE they're available in stores…and they love their *Heart to Heart* subscriber newsletter featuring author news, horoscopes, recipes, book reviews and much more!

5. We hope that after receiving your free books you'll want to remain a subscriber. But the choice is yours — to continue or cancel, any time at all! So why not take us up on our invitation, with no risk of any kind. You'll be glad you did!

YOURS FREE!
This exciting mystery gift is yours free when you play BANGO!

It's fun, and we're giving away
FREE GIFTS
to all players!

The Silhouette Reader Service™ — Here's how it works:

BUSINESS REPLY MAIL

FIRST-CLASS MAIL   PERMIT NO. 717   BUFFALO, NY

POSTAGE WILL BE PAID BY ADDRESSEE

SILHOUETTE READER SERVICE
3010 WALDEN AVE
PO BOX 1867
BUFFALO NY 14240-9952

NO POSTAGE
NECESSARY
IF MAILED
IN THE
UNITED STATES

Chapter Six

"So, tell me, Greg, just how many women *have* you dated?"

The lightness inflected in her voice was meant to let him know she was teasing him. He looked up from the medical journal he was reading, his mouth automatically quirking up at one corner, as sexy as could be. He looked both wary and abashed, obviously unsure of where her comment was coming from…and where it might lead.

The poor man was fatigued to the bone. That much was clear. After putting in his regular office hours, he'd gone to not one, but two medical centers in center city to visit with patients. On top of that, he'd also stopped in at the Wilson Center to see how another of his patients—a young girl with an eating disorder—was responding to treatment and psychological counseling.

He'd called Jane to say he'd be late, so she'd been

prepared. Joy had been fast asleep when Greg had walked through the door at nine. Jane had warmed up his dinner, and after he ate, he went to take a shower while she straightened up the kitchen.

Now he was sitting in the living room reading over some medical magazines. Jane should have gone on to bed and left him alone rather than asking him a question that could turn out to be as lethal as a loaded double-barrel shotgun. But once she'd seen him sit down with that work-related reading material, she hadn't been able to resist offering what she felt would be a much-needed diversion. The man worked too hard.

She offered him one of the two glasses of wine she'd carried in from the kitchen, and he accepted with a silent nod, the sexy grin never leaving his mouth, the uncertainty never leaving his eyes.

Waiting for his answer, she tipped up her glass and sipped the fruity zinfandel.

"So you finally got wind of my reputation, huh?"

His tone might be tentative, but it was also as warm as velvet. Just what a woman wanted on a chilly fall evening.

He laughed lightly. "Who have you been talking to?"

She sat down on the couch next to him. Not wanting to give away her source, she said, "Let's just say a little bird told me."

"Ah." He set aside the magazine and gently swirled the wineglass by the stem. "The infamous little bird." His smile widened. "He can be a dangerous little guy."

Jane's own mouth twisted at the corners. "I promised myself not to believe a word he chirped until I had a chance to ask you myself.''

She'd promised herself no such thing. Asking him anything about his past had never entered her head until she'd seen how tired he'd looked. She'd only meant to take him away from those dry journals he'd planned to read. Get him to relax a bit.

He was silent, the deep green of his eyes reflecting the firelight as he watched her. She took another sip of wine. It warmed her throat as she swallowed, and she realized she felt...odd. Like a lazy cat that felt the need to stretch out languidly and purr.

She shouldn't be sitting here sharing a glass of wine with him in front of the fire. She knew that. During her afternoon walk with Joy, Jane had gone over all the reasons she should ignore the attraction she felt for this man. But the afternoon had been long. The evening, too. And she'd found that she'd missed him today. Was it so bad to want a little human contact? A little adult conversation? A woman could only count and stack blocks and read Little Golden Books for so long before she wanted a little interaction with someone her own age. Was that so wrong?

Sure, there were many reasons why this was wrong. But for the life of her, she couldn't think of even one. This moment felt mysterious and magical, and Jane had experienced so little magic in her life. None, really. She didn't want any doubt or fear to keep her from enjoying every instant of this one.

''That's mighty nice of you,'' he said, ''not to believe any of those awful rumors about me. Birds can be quite malicious when they want to be, you know.''

She chuckled. His tone was as rich and heady as the traces of wine lingering on her tongue, and seemingly more potent. Much more potent. The sound of his voice chased a shiver down her spine. Her skin prickled and the fine hairs on her arms stood on end. Yes. The magic was growing with each passing second.

She didn't understand it. She didn't care to. She simply wanted to relish every wonderful minute.

He took a moment to take a drink, and Jane watched intently as his Adam's apple bobbed with a swallow. She wondered what it might feel like to place a kiss on his jaw now that it was shadowed with a day's growth of mahogany whiskers. Would his light beard feel soft or scratchy against her lips? she wondered. His dark red hair still glistened with dampness from his shower, and she curled her fingers into her palm to keep from reaching out to touch the thick waves.

The urge to connect with him was so strong, so overwhelming. She'd not felt its like in her entire life.

After the firm talking-to she'd given herself this afternoon, she should be clearheaded and logical. She *should* be doing anything else but gazing at him, entertaining these luscious and oh-so-sexy notions welling, swirling, churning inside her. But the ocean swell that had caught her in its powerful current was awesome, and all she wanted to do was ride this enchanting wave to wherever it seemed so determined to take her.

She smiled at him, and the idea that she was flirting should have made her furiously embarrassed. But she wasn't.

"Well," she said, hearing the husky quality in her tone and feeling almost startled that such a seductive sound could emanate from her own throat, "I do like to give a man the chance to explain himself."

He sighed. "I do have to admit it. I've dated a lot of women." His gaze settled on the rim of his glass, then he looked at her. "You know, this society teaches us—males, I mean—as boys and young men to look at females almost as if they were a…a banquet table. And we're encouraged to try as many different dishes as we can. Girls, on the other hand, are taught to…to…"

"Diet?" Jane chuckled, and so did he.

"Maybe food wasn't the best metaphor of choice."

Reaching up, she combed her fingers through her hair. "Good metaphor or not, I understand what you mean."

"It's in the movies. It's on TV. It's in *New York Times* bestselling novels. It's in magazine advertisements. Men are actually *urged* to be ravenous. We're made to feel as if it's our right to reach out and pluck fruit from any tree we desire."

Oh, how she wished he would feel ravenous for her! The mere idea caused her blood to heat. This feeling rolling over her was so new, so exciting! She wanted to be desired.

She grinned at him. "So it's society's fault."

"No, no." He shook his head. "I take full responsibility for my own actions. I just wish I'd learned sooner that...that..."

He seemed at a loss for words, so she supplied, "That women aren't fruit trees meant to satiate the appetites of men?"

His face expressed a mixture of guilt and sheepish embarrassment that Jane found quite endearing.

"I didn't bring this up to make you feel bad," she said. "Lots of women look at men—at life—with the same 'banquet table' mentality. My mother was one of them."

The words tumbled off her tongue without thought, shocking her. Then a thought whizzed through her head, *your sister is another.*

She noticed that he'd grown still, obviously waiting for her to explain. What harm would it do to tell him a little of the truth about her own past? Just so long as she was very careful not to mention Pricilla.

"See, there were men always coming and going in my mother's life." She moistened her lips. "My sister and I had different fathers. Our mother wasn't a very smart woman. She was either too stupid, or too drunk, to protect herself against pregnancy." Jane paused, expecting the old anger to raise its ugly head. But all she felt was numb when she thought about her mother. "She didn't want the responsibility of me or my sister. That was quite clear from the very beginning. So as soon as I was old enough to work, she took off and left us. I haven't seen her for years. And that's okay. We're better off without her in our lives."

She thought of Pricilla. Of how much her sister took after their mother. It wasn't as if this was a new idea to her. But actually explaining their mother's life-style out loud and in her own words, Jane found herself wondering. She'd thought about searching for Pricilla often since coming here. She'd pondered lots of different ways of going about the task. But now she questioned whether or not she should even try to locate her sister. Maybe Pricilla—like her mother—was better off left to her own devices.

Suddenly, she was aware of three things. The first was the heat coming from the fireplace. Second, was the quiet. Third, was the intensity infused in Greg's green eyes. His gaze was just as intimate and arousing as the physical touch of his fingertips on her hot skin would have been.

She blinked. Tucked her bottom lip between her teeth. Then, after inhaling deeply, she drained the wine in her glass.

"I'm awfully sorry." Her voice was quiet now. Terribly quiet. "I didn't mean to bring up my morbid past." She tried to lighten the mood with a laugh, but the sound fell flat. "I only meant to razz you a little about your reputation."

The air was so tight, she thought she'd surely strangle. If he didn't stop looking at her with that deep concern she was going to literally fall to pieces. No one had ever cared about her as much as he seemed to at this moment.

"If you don't mind, I think I'll go to bed now." She made to rise, but he reached out and circled her wrist with his warm fingers. Immediately, she felt sheltered. Cherished. It might be silly. But that's what she felt. It might even be the wine. But that's still what she felt.

"Wait," he whispered.

He pulled her back toward him, and she simply didn't have it in her to resist him.

"I think it's commendable that you took care of yourself and your sister."

She offered him a small, embarrassed smile and murmured, "Thanks." It was very considerate of him to focus on the positive and not bring up her mother's behavior.

"I'm not just being polite," he told her. "I'm serious. You're a very…admirable person. Tell me more. How old were you when you were forced to take over as head of your household?"

He seemed genuinely interested. And Jane felt flattered by the attention. But he was getting too close to the truth. If she began talking in too much detail about her life with Pricilla, she just might slip up. She just might ruin everything. She couldn't risk her place here with Joy. She just couldn't. No matter how much she might want to be honest with him. Now just wasn't the time to tell him the truth.

His eyes were as green as a lush, shady knoll, and she wanted desperately to become lost in their cool, comforting depths. His hand was still on her forearm. And all of a sudden she was ultraconscious of how his thumb was roving slowly, back and forth, across her skin.

Feeling unable to safely reveal any more about her past to him, she could think of only one way to distract him from his query.

She kissed him.

She tasted of wine, heated and honey-sweet. He inhaled slowly, pulling the erotic scent of her deep into his lungs. His hand slid up her arm, over the delicate curve of her shoulder. He wrapped her in his arms and gently tugged her against him.

He'd waited—*hoped*—for this kiss for what had seemed an eternity. Although only two-and-a-half short weeks had passed since she'd come to live in his home, he felt he knew this woman. She was kind. Strong minded. Capable. And she was loving.

Attraction had fairly pulsated between them for days and days. However, he'd been adamant that he would not be the first to outwardly react to the vibrating current. He refused to behave in a fashion that might leave Jane feeling used or exploited. He'd made a silent pledge to allow her the freedom to make the first move—or not to make any move at all. The effort of not reaching out to her, not acting on the awesome, mind-blowing urges that had plagued him like some medieval torture, had been the hardest thing he'd ever done in his life.

But he was glad he'd succeeded in suppressing his desire for her. On account of his restraint, he now knew she was in his arms, kissing his lips, because she *wanted* to be doing these things and not because she'd been wooed or pursued or blindsided by him. For some odd reason, this information caused small explosions of joy to burst in his head, in his gut.

Her lips were hot and moist on his, and he felt passion well in him, filling every nook and cranny, every crevice and fissure of his being, until he thought he'd surely drown in his need of her. But he must contain the overwhelming emotions, the gargantuan hunger. He wanted Jane to be in charge of

the moment. He must let her be the one to take this—
to take *him*—wherever it was she wanted to go.

His whole body literally quaked when she pressed
the first kiss against his throat. His heart thumped
against his rib cage like a jackhammer pummeling
cement pavement. With her heavenly scent wafting
all around him, the taste of her on his tongue, the
feel of her skin under his fingertips, Greg was certain
his senses could want for nothing more.

Then a tiny groan escaped from her throat…and
he trembled at the sound of it.

Never before had he responded to a woman the
way he was responding to Jane. Desire for her filled
every cell of his being, and he didn't know how long
he could control himself.

"Jane," he whispered, his voice jagged as broken
glass. "Oh, heaven help me."

Like some tiny miracle, the wineglass was no
longer in his right hand, and he reached out, sliding
his fingers up her back, driving them deep into her
thick, silken hair. He wanted desperately to press her
mouth against his neck, but he didn't. He wanted to
guide her lips back to meet his once again. But he
didn't. It was very important to him that Jane be in
complete control. And she seemed to revel in the
dominating.

That was quite all right…because he was thoroughly enjoying this new experience of being dom-
inated.

She gave his earlobe a playful nip, and he stifled
a groan. But when she took that same lobe into her
mouth, brushed it with her hot tongue, his breath left
him in a rush and he half murmured, half growled

her name. Her hands seemed to be everywhere at once: sliding up the length of his chest, kneading his shoulder, pressing against his jaw, teasing his thigh.

These were not the caresses of an expert, but rather the eager touch of a kid in a candy store who wanted to see, to feel, to taste *everything*. And he loved the idea of being Jane's sweet.

She drew her feet beneath her on the couch and slid her firm, rounded fanny onto his lap, her mouth never losing contact with his skin. Greg's eyes went wide with surprise, and he feared she would surely feel the evidence of his desire.

He cradled his arms around her, returned her kisses as well as her nibbles. Long, luscious moments were spent with their mouths locked together, their tongues swirling and swaying in that ageless, primal dance of passion. And just as he'd feared, her own eyes opened wide with astonishment when she finally became cognizant of the hardness of him that no amount of restraint could conquer.

"Oh, my," she breathed. "Oh. Oh." She swallowed, tentatively reaching up to touch her moist, kiss-swollen lips. "Oh, my. What have I done? What was I thinking?"

As she asked herself the horrified, whispery questions, she lifted herself from his lap and scooted back down onto the sofa next to him. Her cheeks burned a bright red, clear evidence that, had she the strength, she'd have fled to her room. But her upper body seemed to tremble like a newborn butterfly that found its wings heavy, awkward, cumbersome.

"It's okay." He knew she needed the reassurance, and he slid his hand down her upper arm.

She shuddered delectably, and then she swiped her palm against her damp forehead.

"I'm sorry," she said. "So sorry. I shouldn't have let—"

"Please," he said, cutting her off quickly. "Don't you dare apologize."

She stammered, "B-but…but I never meant to…"

The remainder of her sentence trailed off into oblivion when he released a good-natured groan and grinned at her. "Don't say that, either."

"B-but I work for you, Greg."

Her stutter was so darned cute. Before this moment, he'd never have guessed her to be the nervous kind. She was always so competent. So confident. This uncertainty…this shyness…was just too precious for words.

"I…I…" Again she faltered. "I don't want to— I *can't* do anything to mess up this job. You don't know how important it is."

Then what looked to be panic flared in her eyes, and Greg chuckled in the hope of calming her.

"You're not messing up your job," he told her. "Believe me."

His words didn't seem to relieve her anxiety one iota. Her gaze darted from him, to the fire, back to him, and then to the coffee table.

She was so beautiful. So wholesome. So damned desirable. If her perfect white teeth didn't release the grip they had on her bottom lip, he was certain he was going to have to do one of two things—either grab her up and kiss her soundly, or lose every ounce of his sanity.

"Oh, no!"

His gaze followed hers, and he saw that he'd dropped his wineglass, the rose-hued zinfandel staining the cream-colored carpet. Before he could stop her, she darted up from the sofa and raced toward the kitchen. After only a moment, she was back with a damp towel and blotting at the small discoloration.

"This is all my fault," she said.

He reached down and took her arm. "It's not your fault, Jane. It was my glass. I was the one who dropped it." But for the life of him, he couldn't remember doing it. "Come up here." He tugged at her arm until she once again sat beside him. "Don't worry about the stain. I'll have someone come take care of it."

Once she was settled beside him, he took the soiled towel from her hand and set it aside. Then he clasped both her hands in his. "You're upset by what just happened."

"I've never...*ever*—"

Whatever she'd been about to say embarrassed her into another blushing spree. Her throat convulsed in a tight swallow, and when she spoke next, her voice was barely a whisper.

"I attacked you, Greg. I'm...I'm sorry."

She looked away from him, obviously disconcerted beyond measure. His heart melted in his chest. She was so unlike any other woman he'd ever met. He felt this staggering urge to scoop her up in his arms. To protect her from this awkwardness she was feeling.

She was terribly confident, that showed every day in her tasks as Joy's nanny. But at this moment she wore vulnerability as if it were a gauzy sheath draped from the top of her head to the tips of her toes. She was an enigma that intrigued him to no end.

Keeping his voice low and steady, he said, "And I've already asked you not to apologize. I wanted this…enjoyed this just as much as you."

Suddenly, her shoulders squared, her spine straightened as she evidently forced herself to look him in the eyes.

"I want you to know," she began, "that I don't expect anything from you. I'm not looking for some lifelong commitment from you. I know you're used to fun and frivolity in your…friendships."

Greg felt his brow furrow deeply. He murmured, "I thought you weren't going to listen to rumors." But she didn't seem to hear.

"I can't explain why I—" She stopped, pursed her lips, took a shaky breath. "I don't know why I kissed you like that. But I can promise you that I'm not looking for any kind of…of relationship." She pulled her hands free of his then and hurried from the room.

Long minutes ticked by as he sat there, motionless. The logs in the hearth snapped and sparked as they were consumed by the flames, but he was barely aware of the sounds.

He was bothered by her parting remark. But then, *bothered* was too mild a word to describe the heaviness in his chest. *Disturbed* would better characterize how he was feeling.

Now, if he could only figure out why.

Chapter Seven

"**Y**ou did it, didn't you?"

Greg looked at Travis, confused by his partner's accusatory expression and tone. "Did what?" he asked.

"You crossed the line."

This time it was Sloan who made the charge. Greg felt as if he were being ganged up on. But then, he'd known these men a long time, they were his friends, and it wasn't the first time two of them had teamed against a third. He'd done so himself. Many times. Any time two of them came to the conclusion that the third was headed for some kind of trouble, they didn't hesitate to butt their noses into one another's business. That's what made them such good friends.

But somehow, this time was different. Greg felt Sloan and Travis were out of line. For although he wasn't sure what they were censuring him about, he had a strong feeling Jane's name was about to pop into the conversation.

"Crossed what line?" he asked, his tone tight. Before either of them could answer, Greg continued, "Look, it's too early in the morning to be reprimanded. This is a business meeting. Let's talk business. Anyone have a patient situation that needs discussing?"

Travis snickered. "When have we ever spent our business meetings discussing just business? And don't think you can hornswoggle us into not talking about the trouble you're in—"

"Hornswoggle?" Sloan laughed out loud.

"Hey!" Travis cut his eyes at Sloan, obviously affronted. "It's a word. Look it up. Besides, you're supposed to be on my side in this."

"I am on your side," Sloan assured him.

"If you guys are quite through with the slapstick," Greg said, "I'd like to know what trouble you think I'm in so we can get this out of the way and talk about the important issues. Such as our practice."

"There he goes." Travis eyed Sloan pointedly.

"Yep," Sloan murmured. "He's trying to hornswoggle us again."

Greg only heaved a huge, long-suffering sigh. When these guys had a bone to pick, there was no moving on until it was picked clean.

"Okay," Greg said. "Out with it. What did I do? What line did I cross? What has your noses out of joint this time?"

Travis and Sloan exchanged a quick glance, and then Travis leveled his gaze on Greg.

"You slept with her, didn't you?"

"*Slept with—*"

"Don't try to deny it," Sloan cut in. "We can tell something has happened between you and Jane. We know you, remember." A subtle yet substantial change invaded his voice as he added, "We know you well."

Again, Sloan and Travis shared a look…a knowing look that caused Greg's blood pressure to skyrocket.

"And what is that supposed to mean?" His tone was low and ominous. Yes, these men were his best friends in the whole world. But a man could only take so much antagonism before he began to feel like a cornered dog, snarling and ready to bite back.

"Don't give us that," Travis said.

Sloan added, "You know exactly what we mean."

Neither man seemed the least bit intimidated by Greg's anger. In fact, both their gazes twinkled with the kind of merriment that didn't need words to explain *exactly* what they thought of his display of outrage.

His shoulders sagged a fraction. Who was he kidding? Travis and Sloan *did* know him. Better than anyone else. And their concern for him was just that—honest concern for a friend. He ought to be grateful for the interest and worry they so willingly invested in him and the happenings of his life. The last thing he should be is angry with them.

"Look," he said, "I didn't sleep with Jane, okay?"

They stared at him in silence, then exchanged dubious expressions.

"I didn't!" he insisted. "I know, given my past history, that you might find that hard to believe. But it's the truth. On my honor."

Sloan murmured to Travis, "Does the man have enough honor left that we can believe him?"

Holding his index finger and thumb about an inch apart, Travis said, "I guess he's got just enough left in him to make him relatively believable."

Greg had two choices. He could laugh. Or punch his best friends in their ornery faces here and now.

He laughed. He prized their friendship too much to do anything else.

"Okay," Sloan said, "so you didn't sleep with the woman. But you did cross the line, didn't you? The two of you have become something more than merely employer and employee."

"You kissed her," Travis said. He didn't form the words as a question, seeming to already know the answer.

After a moment, Greg leaned back in his chair, reached up and raked his fingers though his hair. "What? Are you guys peeking through my windows or something?"

"We don't have to." Sloan picked up a ballpoint pen from the conference tabletop and began to twist the lid. "We work with you everyday."

Travis just chuckled. Then both men's gazes sobered and Travis pressed his elbows on the table, leaning toward Greg. "Have you lost your mind?" he asked. "That woman is working for you."

"I know. I know." Greg scrubbed his face with both palms. "But, look, you've got to believe me when I tell you that I wasn't the instigator. She was. *She* kissed *me*."

Two pairs of eyebrows shot skyward in surprise.

"You expect us to believe that Jane made the first move on you, the Casanova of Philadelphia?" The pen stilled in Sloan's fingers.

"I expect you to believe me. Because it's the truth."

The three of them were silent for a moment. Worried that his friends might get the wrong idea about the situation, Greg said, "But she's not interested in a relationship."

"Whoa," Travis said. "So our Jane's turned out to be a party girl, has she?"

But one narrow-eyed look from Greg and Travis was sputtering an apology. "I was just joking, Greg. Just teasing you. Don't be so touchy. I didn't mean a thing."

"Well, why would she come on to you if she's not interested in a relationship?" Sloan had set the pen down now, his gaze focused, his brow furrowed.

Greg heaved a sigh. "She got caught up in the moment?" He shook his head. "I've been going around and around trying to figure it out, myself. It's very…upsetting."

"What's upsetting?" Travis asked softly. "The fact that you're now on the receiving end of the same kind of treatment you've doled out to women for years?"

His eyes going wide with astonishment, Greg sat there speechless for several seconds. "You think that's what has me feeling so troubled about…Jane and what happened between us? I never thought

about it like that. I've been an—'' he searched the
air for the correct word ''—instigator for a very long
time. I've kissed a lot of women the same way Jane
kissed me—''

''Yes, but the one difference is,'' Sloan pointed
out, ''those women made it clear that they *wanted*
to be kissed, right?'' He shot Greg a narrowed
glance. ''You haven't been coming on to the woman,
have you?''

''No.'' Greg shook his head adamantly. Then he
admitted, ''I *have* felt attracted to her.''

''Of course you have,'' Travis murmured. ''She's
a woman, isn't she? And you're...well, you're
Greg.''

A dirty look was Greg's only response.

Then, Greg continued, ''But I promised myself—
no, I *forced* myself to ignore what I felt. I need
Jane's help with Joy. I didn't want to do anything to
mess that up. I told myself that if anything were to
happen, it would have to be at her prompting—''

''Oh, man,'' Sloan groaned.

''*What?*'' Greg threw his hands up in the air.
''What's so wrong about that?''

''If you felt attracted to the woman, she was going
to know. Women have a sixth sense about these
things.'' Sloan shook his head, lacing his fingers together. ''I can't help but point out that, after all this
time, you still know very little about this woman.
Did you ever hear from her sister, like she promised?''

Greg's lips drew together tightly. Why did they
insist on asking difficult questions? Questions he

didn't care to answer. But he knew he had to. Sloan only had his best interest at heart.

"No," he answered quietly.

He thought about how well he'd come to know Jane, and how good she was with his daughter, how loving and giving. Suddenly, Sloan's suspicion seemed silly.

"I'll tell you what I think," Greg said, a sudden tenseness straining his words. "Jane and her sister are notorious bank robbers. I haven't heard from her sister because the two of them pulled the job of the century and they're both in hiding. Her sister can't call me, see, because the federal government has my phone bugged."

Surely now his friends would have no trouble understanding what he thought of their continued mistrust of Jane.

"Na, that can't be it." Travis's tone was just as serious as the day was long. "If Jane had robbed a bank she'd be sitting on the beach of some tropical island right now sipping a cool, frothy drink from a coconut shell, not laundering Greg's smelly T-shirts, washing his dirty dishes and baby-sitting his ten-month-old baby girl."

"My T-shirts do not smell," Greg commented.

"Yeah," Travis said, "and I can recommend a good doctor who'll be happy to check out your nose, 'cause it don't seem to be working."

The men sat in silence, and finally Travis laughed. Greg couldn't help but crack a smile.

"You two joke all you want," Sloan said, refusing to join in the joviality. "But you mark my words, something isn't right with that woman. She's not being completely honest about something."

Greg stood up and reached for the files he'd set on the table upon entering the meeting. "I have to tell you, Sloan, your suspicions are wearing a bit thin." He tapped the edges of the folders on the table to straighten them. "If you're coming to Thanksgiving dinner, then you should know that Jane's going to be there. And I don't want you saying anything that might hurt her feelings, or have her thinking that you don't like her."

Why was he acting so damned protective? The irritation pumping through his veins kept him from delving too deeply into whatever answer he might have for the question.

Finally, he said, "You guys have a good day. I'm outta here. I have patient files to update."

With that said, he left the room.

He'd just closed his office door when there was a tap on it. Greg opened it to find the office manager standing there.

"Hi, Rachel," he said.

He frowned when the woman didn't return her usual smile of greeting.

"Can I come in a minute, Greg?" she asked.

"Sure." He ushered her inside and closed the door. "Is there a problem? One of the nurses giving you trouble? Someone give their notice?"

"No, no, nothing like that." She reached up and tucked a strand of blond hair behind her ear. "But there is something…"

"What is it? I'll help you work it out if I can." Greg's brows drew together. Rachel was efficient and highly motivated. A problem solver. It was rare that she came to the partners with a complaint or a problem, and when she did, she usually called a meeting so that all the partners were included.

"I, um," she began hesitantly, "I couldn't help overhearing a little of what went on just now in the meeting."

Greg groaned. "Oh, not you, too, Rachel. Look, I'm getting enough flack about Jane from Travis and Sloan—"

She stopped him with a firm shake of her head. "No, I wasn't going to say a word against your new nanny. I've seen Jane with Joy. She's wonderful with that baby. The only advice I can give you there is to follow your heart. Listen to what your heart tells you, and you can't go wrong."

Then she averted her eyes. "But—" again she hesitated, her gaze returning to his face "—I, um, I was going to ask you to have a little patience with Sloan."

Thinking about Sloan's behavior this morning, how he continued to doubt Jane like a hound dog on a scent, Greg frowned. "What's wrong with Sloan, Rachel?"

"Well, he's having some problems at home."

Immediately, Sloan's set of triplet daughters flashed into his mind. "The girls? One of them sick?"

"No, nothing like that." Rachel absently toyed with the upper corner of the stack of insurance forms she cradled in one arm. "Just a few…growing pains. But Sloan is stressed out about it. I just thought you should know."

Greg was silent a moment. "It's awfully nice of you to tell me."

Color tinged her cheeks, and Greg saw her emotions just as clearly as if they had been words spelled out on a blackboard. He wanted to tell the woman to stay away from poker tables. She'd never successfully conceal a good hand of cards.

Finally, he reached out and touched Rachel's forearm. "You know," he said softly, "that advice you just gave me, the stuff about listening to your heart and following it? Those are...very wise words to live by."

Her face flooded with heated embarrassment.

"Sloan sure could use a friend—"

"Please—" she cut him off "—I really do have tons of work to do. And you don't pay me to stand around talking about...personal issues." With that said, she turned, pulled open the door and bolted.

Alone in his office once more, Greg sat down at his desk feeling as if he'd already put in a hard day's work rather than just starting one. Was Rachel right? he wondered. Had Sloan's problems with his daughters been the motivating factor behind the suspicions he'd voiced?

Sure, tension at home could have agitated Sloan to the point of being grouchy. He could have been using Greg's situation with Jane as a way of venting his own frustrations with parenthood. Sloan sure had refused to back down in his suspicions about Jane. But Greg had to admit that his friend had raised a valid concern.

That darned phone call. The one that had yet to come from Jane's sister. It had been weeks now. He should confront Jane about it. He knew that. But he just plain didn't have the heart to.

Cradling his forehead in his fingers, he wondered why. Why didn't he want to challenge Jane about the promised call?

"Because she just might turn out to be a bank robber," he whispered to the walls of his empty office.

"You're a real gem for helping me with dinner."

Jane walked next to the grocery store cart that Greg pushed, grinning down at where little Joy sat, safely secured by a tether belt, in the front seat. "I'm happy to help. In fact, I'm looking forward to it."

She couldn't put into words just how pleased she was to be spending Thanksgiving Day with Greg and Joy. Getting to know his friends was going to be like icing on a delicious birthday cake.

Even though it was dangerous to be thinking this way, she couldn't help but realize how much she and Greg and Joy seemed like an honest-to-goodness family unit. Mom. Dad. Child. The mere thought made her smile.

"What has you grinning?" Greg asked her.

"Oh, nothing."

Greg happily reminisced. "My mom always had a house full of people in for the holidays. Every holiday. Friends, neighbors. We didn't have any close relatives—Mom and Dad were both only children—but the rooms always seemed to burst at the seams."

He closed his eyes, evidently engulfed in the past, and Jane's gaze riveted to his handsome face.

"And the smells coming from the kitchen." He inhaled. "Wonderful."

The past wasn't something she wanted to talk about, so she tried changing the subject. "Well, I can't promise to equal your mother's cooking. If that's what you're looking for, we'd better rush out and find a good caterer."

Greg chuckled. "Nah. We'll do just fine on our own. I'm kinda looking forward to cooking with you."

He captured her with those gorgeous green eyes of his, and Jane was certain her knees were going to give out on her.

"It'll be fun."

She didn't know what to say. It would be fun. It would be exciting and wonderful. But she didn't dare voice her feelings for fear of coming across as too eager. Pathetic and pitiful. So she simply offered him a closemouthed smile.

He chose a five-pound bag of flour from the shelf and placed it into the cart. "So, you never did tell me..."

"What?"

"What had you smiling," he said. "What kind of memories do you have of Thanksgiving?"

Her chest constricted. "Actually," she began slowly, "I wasn't remembering. There isn't much about my past to smile about."

Careful, a voice warned from the back of her brain.

"You see," she continued, "my past consists of two periods—life before Mom left, and life after Mom left. Before she left, holidays were pretty dreary. No money. Little food. I had to deal with two things…three, really—Mom's drinking, her men friends, and protecting Pr—''

She choked off the name and ended up trying to cover her blunder with a cough. Lord above! She'd nearly spoken her sister's name.

Details mean trouble, the voice in her head taunted.

''And—and protecting my sister from the whole mess.'' In a rush, she proceeded, ''You see, my mother had a way of making us feel to blame for her dreadful circumstances.''

Suddenly, Jane felt shaky, sure that she was going to trip over something and the truth was going to come spilling out. Why had she felt compelled to pour out her troubled past to Greg?

''Life after Mom wasn't much better. Money was still tight. Tight enough to make special holiday meals impossible. However, I didn't have to deal with Mom's drunkenness, or her men friends, or the guilt she piled on our shoulders.'' One corner of her mouth cocked upward and she shook her head. ''I spent the very first Thanksgiving after my mom left in the hospital. I was walking home from work late and was hit by a car. I had internal injuries and I was pretty bruised up, but my greatest fear was that Social Services would find my sister home alone and take her away. But, you know, no one ever asked a single question about my family.''

She frowned, her voice sounding far off as she continued, ''Once the hospital administrators discovered I was eighteen with no health insurance and no money, they patched me up as well as they could and got me out of there in just under a week."

Jane would live with the effects of the car accident for the rest of her life. Suddenly realizing the past had somehow folded in on her, she blinked and tried to smile. She was mortified by the expression she saw on his face.

"Now, don't go pitying me," she chided him. "I know what Thanksgiving is all about. And I've spent every Thanksgiving Day since then appreciating the good things in my life."

"And what are those?"

His question was soft as heated silk. Interested. Totally absorbed with obvious concern for her, and Jane felt enveloped in the warmth he exuded.

"I'm thankful for my mom."

This answer seemed to take him aback.

She nodded. "Really. Because of her, I was forced to take care of myself. I'm independent. I'm self-reliant. I'm fully capable of getting by on my own. If I'd have been born into some other family, I may have grown up soft. And needy."

Right there in the middle of the supermarket aisle, Greg inched closer to her. With his gaze so intent, so focused on her, Jane felt as if they were the only two people in the world. He reached up and stroked the length of her jaw with the backs of his fingers.

"You're really something, you know that?"

A shiver raced up her spine at his touch…at the base of her neck it exploded and coursed across every inch of her flesh in pinpricks, like millions of tiny stars rolling end-over-end across her skin.

"But I have to tell you—" his tone was low, intimate "—there are times when it's good to be soft and needy. There are times when we really, *really* need to rely on others."

She felt as if he were looking into the very depths of her soul. If his gaze got any hotter, she'd surely melt right where she stood. If she didn't do something to diminish the intensity of this moment, she didn't know what would happen, what she might say, what she might reveal to this wonderful man.

Reaching up, she curled her fingers around his wrist. "But for some of us, Greg, there isn't anyone to rely on but ourselves."

Her attempt to lessen the momentousness of the situation failed miserably. For, upon hearing her reply, his expression only seemed to grow more profound, more meaningful.

Without another word, he bent and covered her mouth with his. Taken aback by the unexpected contact, all she could do was stand there. No, that's not true. She didn't just stand there. She closed her eyes, lifted herself up on her toes.

His kiss was filled with warmth. It was also filled with an undeniable message.

He was offering himself, she realized. He was attempting to convey to her that he was someone on whom she could rely.

When he pulled back to gaze once again into her eyes, her lips felt chilled.

Jane didn't know what to say. Didn't know what to do.

"Ma, mmm, ma."

The baby's excited tone had both Jane and Greg stepping apart, turning their attention to Joy.

The child motioned to Jane, waving her hand and mouthing, "Ma, ma, ma, ma, ma."

"Looks like she's trying to get your attention," Greg said, grinning at his daughter's cute antics.

But Jane was so overwhelmed by the sound of her niece's voice that she couldn't tear her eyes away from Joy's face. Jane knew Joy wasn't saying what it sounded like she was saying. A baby had to be instructed how to say the word *mama*. A child had to be *taught* to physically form the word. And never once in all the months Jane had been caring for Joy had she presumed to say that word to Joy. But it sure sounded as if...

Hot tears sprang forth, welling in Jane's eyes, splintering her vision into shards of bright light. Fate may have dealt her a vicious blow when it came to motherhood, but her maternal instinct was just as strong as that of any normal woman. And any normal woman who cared for a child—her own child— would be overcome at a moment like this.

Never in her life had she imagined a child calling her mother. Never. She simply hadn't allowed herself to contemplate it. And even though she knew full well that the baby really wasn't calling her mother, Jane still felt thunderstruck by emotion as Joy reached out to her, as she heard the baby making those wonderful sounds.

"Ma, mmm, ma!" Joy giggled, obviously delighted that she'd gotten Jane's attention. Then the baby reached her chubby little hand, wiggling her fingers at the floor.

"What, baby? What is it?" Jane crooned, her voice sounding weak, thinned by the emotion flood-

ing through her. "Oh, you've dropped your rattle."
She automatically reached to pick it up. But rather
than give it back to Joy, she stuffed it in the diaper
bag and searched for something else to give to the
baby. "That one's dirty," she told Joy. "Let's look
for something else to play with."

She spent a minute searching in the bag. She
needed time to garner her wits about her. What
would Greg think if he saw her bawling simply because Joy had called out to her? He'd think her utterly ridiculous.

Jane chatted with Joy as she gently urged the cart
forward. The business of shopping for groceries for
the Thanksgiving feast was once again the focus of
the moment, and for that Jane was relieved.

That kiss. The look he'd given her. The silent
message he'd imparted. Her relationship with Greg
was developing into something she'd never imagined
she'd have.

He was wonderful. Warm and witty. It was hard
to describe in mere words how amazing he was. Just
thinking about him made her skin prickle all over.

She cast him a furtive look, and then glanced
down at Joy. Oh, my, how they did seem to make a
fine family, the three of them.

Her heart ached as she realized they would never
become a family. There was something standing in
the way of that ever happening.

A huge, ugly lie.

Chapter Eight

Bad things were so easy to forget. Guilt could be so effortlessly ignored. Lies were so easy to push aside. Especially when the excitement of a holiday was at hand.

A coating of frost covered the trees and bushes outside Jane's window when she awoke and got herself dressed on Thanksgiving morning. She would be spending the day with Greg and his friends, and she was thrilled with the idea. Her wardrobe was simple, but she did own a red tunic sweater that could pass for festive apparel even if it was a little worn. So she tugged it over her head, slipped on a pair of black knit leggings and slid her feet into black loafers.

A touch of mascara highlighted her gray-blue eyes, and lipstick—something she seldom wore—accentuated her mouth. She gazed in the mirror as she ran the brush through her honey brown hair and thought she didn't look half bad for the "one who had inherited the brains rather than the looks."

She couldn't help but think that her attitude had a lot to do with the change in how she felt about her appearance. Funny how a man's attention could shift a woman's whole way of thinking about herself.

Chuckling, she went out to meet the day.

"Wow!"

Greg's voice stopped her in her tracks as she came through the kitchen doorway.

"You look fabulous."

Heat flushed her cheeks and her stomach danced with nerves. It was a pleasant feeling. Nice. Tingly. And she smiled.

"Thanks," she murmured. "I'm really excited about getting to know your friends. How soon before we start cooking?"

"I've set dinner for three o'clock."

"That early?"

Greg grinned. "Yes. It's a Thanksgiving tradition around here to eat in the afternoon, which paves the way for an eight o'clock snack." His mouth twisted with humor. "That way everyone gets to enjoy their favorite dishes twice."

"Sounds like a good tradition to me."

Any tradition at all would have been okay with Jane. She'd grown up with no customs whatsoever. She'd have eaten a breakfast of turkey, stuffing, mashed potatoes and gravy while standing on her head if that's what Greg had wanted to do. It felt marvelous just to be included in this extremely family-oriented day.

She knew, from the way he'd spoken of his friends

and partners, Sloan and Travis, that the men were like family to him. In fact, since Greg had no family, these men were the closest thing to it he had. Jane liked the way the three men had banded together because they had no real family support. She'd discovered from Greg that Travis had a mother and brother, but that there was some kind of rift that kept them apart. Jane didn't know much about Sloan's family, or lack thereof, but she hoped to learn more about him. He was supposed to be bringing his three girls to the dinner. And Rachel, their office manager, was invited also. So being included in this event had Jane feeling absolutely ecstatic. This would be the closest thing to a family gathering she'd ever attended.

Wanting all of Greg's friends to like her, she was willing to do whatever it took to see that the meal—the whole day—turned out perfectly.

"So we should put the turkey in soon, don't you think?" she asked.

"I had hoped to get the bird in the oven before Joy woke up." He pulled a mug down from the shelf. "I'm happy to have your help," he said as he poured coffee, "but you haven't even had your dose of caffeine yet."

He was so sweet to think of her. She took the mug from his hands. "I do use this stuff like medicine, don't I?"

"Hey—" his grin was to-die-for sexy "—you're not alone in that." Then he lifted his own mug in a kind of salute, and then they settled in to enjoy the morning ritual that millions of people all over the world practiced.

Mmm. The coffee was hot, rich and delicious on her tongue.

The two of them sat at the kitchen table and talked about some of the current news of the day that Greg had read in the morning paper.

Finally, he said, "You want a refill?"

"Oh, no. Thanks, but I'm anxious to get a crack at that bird." Then she cast him a hesitant look. "You don't mind if I prepare the turkey for the oven, do you? I've never cooked for Thanksgiving. As I told you yesterday, when I was a kid, there was never enough money for a nice meal. And then after I started working at the restaurant, I always worked holidays."

"Sure." He seemed more than happy to allow her the honor. "I don't mind in the least. If you want to get your hands dirty, who am I to say no?"

He chuckled, and Jane had to fight the urge to close her eyes in order to get lost in the wonderful sound of it. He was kind and caring to everyone around him, and there simply didn't seem to be a discontented bone in the man's body.

"But will you help me?" she quickly asked. "I will need a little instruction since I've never done this before. I do want the main course to be edible."

Tipping his handsome face to one side, he bowed. "I'll be right here. At your service."

They looked at each other. In the silence, his words seemed to swell and grow and take up all the extra room in the kitchen. The air suddenly felt close. The temperature heated up.

Drawing her bottom lip between her teeth, Jane studied Greg's gaze. And he studied hers.

His soft smile broke the trance that had her securely ensnared.

"We'd better get a move on," he said softly. "Joy will be stirring any minute."

Reluctantly, she got up from the table and moved to the sink to wash her hands.

"Here," he said, taking one elbow, "let me help you."

Then he tugged on the sleeve of her sweater until it was far enough up her forearm to keep it dry. He did the same to her other sleeve.

He was so close she could smell the wonderful scent of him, and every time his fingertips grazed her skin she seemed to become more and more hypersensitive to his touch. Her blood chugged, thick and heated, through her veins.

"Thanks," she said, her voice coming out in a husky whisper. "I should have thought of that myself."

"Well, you can't think of everything all the time."

Something happened to his tone, something extraordinary that sent Jane's heart rate soaring.

"You take such good care of us," he continued. "You keep Joy happy and healthy. You keep the house looking wonderful. And I haven't gone to work in a rumpled lab coat since you came to work for me. So it makes me feel good to be able to help you out. Even if it is only keeping your sleeves dry."

His grin was so sexy it bordered on seductive, and Jane found herself shying away from his gaze. But he reached up, tucked his curled fingers under her chin and applied just enough gentle pressure to force her to look at him.

"I want you to know I appreciate all that you've done for us."

Again, the air in the room seemed to close in on her. She wanted desperately to look into his eyes forever. She wanted just as desperately to look away.

"Now," he murmured, "let's get to that turkey before my daughter wakes up."

Greg made it a practice to cook his stuffing in a casserole dish as opposed to inside the turkey, so he had her season the cavity with salt and pepper and a crushed garlic clove. Then he instructed her to fill the bird with a halved onion, a halved orange and some celery stalks, explaining that the fruit and veggies would keep the meat moist as well as impart a delicious flavor.

He helped her lift the turkey into a huge roasting pan and then he had her smear the outside skin with butter. On top of that, she sprinkled some savory spices. Because Jane's fingers were now a glistening, spicy mess, Greg popped the lid onto the roaster and shoved the pan into the oven.

"We'll start basting in a couple of hours."

She washed the butter from her hands. "Where did you learn all this?"

"How to cook a turkey?" he asked.

"Yes. Don't most bachelors eat out?"

He cast her a wide-eyed, openmouthed look of horror. "Eating Thanksgiving dinner in a restaurant would be sacrilegious!"

Jane laughed at his antics.

As she dried her hands, she heard sounds coming

from the monitor that told her Joy was awake and playing happily in her crib.

"Do you hear that?" she told Greg. And they spent several seconds listening to Joy gurgle and coo to herself.

"You know," Jane said, "no parent could ask for a more good-natured baby."

She was staring at the monitor, so when his mouth descended on hers, she was taken completely by surprise. His kiss was swift, but sound. And when he pulled back from her, she was as wide-eyed as he had been just a moment before.

"I'd like to be able to say that's a thank you," he said, his tone silky, warm and sweet as maple syrup. "I'd like to say it's for loving my daughter as much as I do. But..."

He paused, the sheer intensity of his gaze pinning her to the spot for another moment or two before he continued.

When he did speak, his tone was hushed. "But that would only be half the truth."

And then he left her standing there feeling terribly excited, her thoughts chaotic, as she pondered the meaning behind his words.

Greg's apartment had always seemed large to Jane with its three bedrooms, two bathrooms, formal dining room, large living area and kitchen. But with Travis, Sloan and his nearly teenaged triplets, Rachel, plus Greg, Joy and Jane, the apartment seemed cramped. However, it wasn't unpleasant. Not by any stretch of the imagination. Sloan's daughters played with Joy, read her books and made castles out of wooden blocks for her. The men enjoyed a beer, Rachel and Jane a glass of wine, as everyone talked and laughed and joked together.

These people were so nice, and they treated her well. As if she'd always been one of them.

"So, Travis," Greg said to his friend, "any word on the adoption?"

"Yes."

Travis showed clear signs of his Native American heritage in his piercing coal-black eyes and his prominent and high cheekbones. His hair was longer than what was conventional, but he kept it tied back in a neat ponytail. The man's gaze lit up when Greg asked him about the adoption.

"The council has requested another meeting." Sudden anxiety clouded his handsome features. "I hate to get my hopes up, but I really would like to have Jared and Josh home for Christmas."

"I think it's a wonderful thing that you're doing," Rachel said. "You've spent so much time with the boys…gone out of your way to help them. I don't understand why that…committee, or whatever it is, doesn't see how hard you've worked."

Greg caught Jane's attention. "Travis made it possible for the boys to have heart surgery a few years ago," he told her. "He's kept in touch with them, and now he's decided he'd like to adopt."

"That's marvelous, Travis." She wasn't able to keep the awe out of her voice. Well, that was okay, she figured. He was endeavoring on an awesome task.

Travis smiled. "They're pretty marvelous kids. I just hope the Kolheek Council of Elders will allow me to become the boys' father.'' His gaze scanned them all. ''I'll be leaving for the reservation next week.''

''I'll be happy to cover for you,'' Greg offered.

Sloan added, ''You know I'll pitch in, too.''

Jane felt warm inside. Never in her life had she experienced or even witnessed this kind of closeness between people. Concentrating on simply surviving had kept her from developing any real friends.

Your sister should be a friend. The thought whispered through her head, haunting and painful. But Jane shoved it away. She didn't want to spend one second of this wonderful day pondering regrets.

''Dad?''

Sloan turned to face one of his daughters. When they had first arrived, the girls had introduced themselves, but they looked so much alike, Jane would have been hard-pressed to guess which was Sophie, which was Sydney and which was Sasha. But evidently Sloan didn't have that problem.

''Yes, Sydney?''

''Can we paint the baby's fingernails?'' the girl asked.

''Absolutely not!'' Sloan stood, a frown marring his brow. ''I don't allow you to paint your own fingernails. Why would I allow you to paint Joy's? What are you doing with fingernail polish, anyway?''

''Take a chill pill, Dad,'' Sydney said. ''If you don't want me to do it, I won't.'' She shrugged. ''No big deal.''

''It *is* a big deal, young lady,'' he scolded. ''Bring that bottle of polish to me. Now.''

Sydney did as she was told, heaving a huge, melo-dramatic sigh that only an adolescent on the verge of being a teen could.

Out of Sloan's line of vision, Jane saw one of Sydney's sisters stealthily slip something—Jane sus-pected it was yet another bottle of nail polish—into her small leather shoulder bag. Jane looked at Ra-chel, who seemed to be sending a silent message to the child with an intent "put that away quick" gaze.

"You didn't answer me, young lady," Sloan said. "Where did you get this?"

"I bought it with my allowance."

"Sloan—" Rachel spoke up "—Sydney did ask permission. From me. She bought it when I took the girls shopping this past weekend."

A moment of awkward silence ensued.

Then Sloan softly said, "B-but you were only sup-posed to be looking for those...those hair things—"

"Barrettes, Daddy." Another sigh erupted from Sydney. "Those *hair things* are called barrettes. And I don't see why we can't paint our nails. Rachel made me pick out a light color. We're going to be thirteen in just a couple of months."

"Yeah, Dad," one of the other girls added in.

"Yeah." The third sister stifled a snicker.

Oh, boy, Jane thought. Having one daughter on the threshold of her teen years would be bad enough, but it was clear that Sloan was going to have his hands full with his triplets. Especially when the three of them were obviously smart enough to realize that a unified front was a strong front.

Sloan's handsome features transformed into what could be described in no other way than a "daddy face.'' One eyebrow cocked, lips pursed. The change shouted a silent warning that Jane certainly would have heeded had she been one of the girls. However, none of the children seemed to be the least concerned with or deterred by their father's stern expression.

Sydney continued, ''Geez, all the other girls at school paint their nails *and* wear lip gloss.''

''I'm not concerned with the other girls at school,'' Sloan said, his tone clear evidence that he was doing his utmost to control his response to his daughter's argument. ''First off, Rachel shouldn't have given permission for you to buy the polish without checking with me first.''

Rachel looked utterly miserable. ''I realize that now.'' Her words were nearly whispered. ''And I'm sorry.''

''Don't be mad at Rachel,'' Sydney said, her tone seeming to be nudging toward a battle. ''She's only trying to help us tear free of your control freak clutches.''

With her eyes wide with silent horror, Rachel remained mute as she lifted her hand and pressed her palm to the base of her throat. Sympathy for the woman welled up inside Jane. She wished there was something she could say to alleviate the ever-growing tension of the situation. But she'd just met these people. Didn't know them well enough to butt into their business. Particularly in something as momentous as this—challenged parental control.

Sloan's frown deepened as he looked at his young daughter. Quietly but firmly, he said, ''This is not the place to discuss this.''

"That's right," Greg interjected. "This is a day of celebration. And I think dinner is just about ready. Jane, maybe you, Rachel and the girls can set the table while I make the gravy and check the rolls."

Relief flooded Jane. She could have kissed Greg for diverting everyone's attention. But since she couldn't kiss the man in front of his friends, she settled for sending him a grateful glance.

Greg tossed her a sexy grin and left for the kitchen, enlisting Travis's help. But before Jane could even make a move toward the dining room, she witnessed something extraordinary.

All three of the girls gathered around Sloan, hugging him around the waist.

"Don't be mad at us, Daddy," one of his daughters said, gazing up into his face.

"And don't be mad at Rachel," another one added.

The third pressed her face against her dad's biceps. "We love you, Daddy."

The tension in the air—and on Sloan's face—dissipated as quickly as it had surfaced.

Rachel came to stand within a foot of the father-daughters hug-fest. "And I really am sorry."

Something shone in the woman's eyes…something profound, something that hinted to Jane that Rachel harbored deep feelings for Sloan.

"It's okay," he told Rachel.

The tender concern expressed in the woman's eyes only intensified, but Jane was sure Sloan had missed it, as he'd immediately turned his attention back to his daughters.

"I love you, too," he told the girls. "And I'm not

angry. I just need you to know that…I'm only trying to…''

He sighed as, evidently, the difficult words seemed to fail him.

''I just think your mom would be so upset to know that you guys are trying to…to grow up too quickly.'' He cleared his throat. ''I don't like to think she might be looking down from heaven feeling disappointed in how I'm raising the three of you.''

Jane noticed that several things happened at once: everyone's gazes averted at the mention of the deceased woman, Sloan's voice trailed in a strangle as he grew all misty-eyed, and Rachel suddenly looked distressed beyond measure.

As much as Rachel's face revealed her feelings for Sloan and his girls, it was also just as clear that he seemed oblivious to the woman's feelings for him and the children.

The moment had simply grown too awkward for Jane to bear, and because Greg had already disappeared into the kitchen with Travis, she forced herself to reach out to touch Rachel on the sleeve. Quietly, Jane said, ''Let's go set the table.''

Rachel nodded, and the girls seemed eager to escape the tight and uncomfortable scene that had somehow developed in the living room.

Scooping up Joy into her arms, Jane followed Rachel and the girls into the dining room. However, she couldn't help but feel sorry for Sloan as he stood there all alone with grief that was all too raw and exposed.

Festiveness and fun quickly returned to the afternoon when everyone sat down together at the dinner table. Another great tradition was revealed as each person present was asked by Greg what it was that he or she was most thankful for.

"Well, even though nothing is final yet," Travis was quick to say, "I'm very thankful for the opportunity to try to adopt Josh and Jared." The man's voice softened as he added, "I just hope I have them home by Christmas."

"It'll happen," Greg assured him.

Jane, Sloan and everyone else couldn't keep from nodding in agreement and encouragement.

Rachel softly said, "I'm very grateful for my job. And for the fact that all of you are willing to put up with me during holidays."

"Uh-oh." Greg's tone took on a teasing quality. "Our normally calm, cool and collected office manager is being downright silly."

His laughter had everyone chuckling, too. And he had Rachel coloring prettily.

"We're grateful that you run the office so well, Rachel," Greg said. "Aren't we, guys?"

Travis said, "Absolutely."

Sloan merely smiled and nodded.

Jane wanted to smack Sloan for not complimenting Rachel when he had this perfect chance. The man's head must be thick as concrete.

"And as for us putting up with you," Greg continued. "Well, I say you're one of the family. Right, everyone?"

The girls shouted "Yes!" in unison and then broke up into gales of laughter.

"I'm grateful for my giggling girls," Sloan said,

"How about you, Sasha? What are you thankful for?"

Sasha had only had a split second to contemplate her answer when one of her sisters shouted, "Sasha's thankful for the telephone."

"Yeah," the other sister concurred. "We're looking into making her life simpler by sewing the receiver to her ear."

Sophie and Sydney shared a look and then snickered at their sibling.

Sasha was clearly incensed. "Well, Sophie, everyone knows you're thankful for Bobby Snyders."

Sophie gasped in horror.

"And Sydney," Sasha continued, "is thankful that Rachel promised to take her shopping for an over-the-shoulder-boulder-holder. Even though she has no boulders yet."

Sydney was just as mortified as Sophie now. Sloan just seemed confused. It was Rachel who cleared up everyone's bewilderment when she silently mouthed the word *bra* to the adults. The color seemed to drain from Sloan's face.

Jane sensed another awkward moment fast approaching. To head it off, she said, "Do I get a chance to be thankful?"

All eyes were on her as she hadn't said much during the meal.

"I am very grateful to be spending this holiday with Joy," Jane said. Emotion welled up from seemingly nowhere, but she plowed ahead. "She is definitely the…light of my life." Looking at Greg, Jane lifted her water glass toward him. "I offer you a toast, Greg. In appreciation. I thank you for allowing me the privilege of being your daughter's nanny.''

"Hear, hear." Travis raised his glass, too. And, one by one, so did everyone else.

They sipped to Jane's toast, and when things settled down once more, it was Greg's turn to speak.

He began slowly, his voice quavering with emotion. "I think I'm more thankful this year than in any year past. I have a daughter. A gorgeous baby who has changed my whole life for the better. And for her—for Joy—I am more appreciative than words can express.''

Travis and Sloan refused to allow their friend to bask in this somber moment for long. After just a couple seconds, they razzed him something fierce about his sentimentality. Greg absorbed the good-natured ribbing with humor, and soon the table broke up into several smaller conversations as everyone began enjoying their dinner.

The turkey was succulent, the mashed potatoes smooth and rich with butter, the stuffing, delicious. Sloan fussed at the girls for playing with their food, and Travis and Rachel talked about some work-related topic.

Greg curled his fingers around Jane's wrist and leaned close to her. For her ears alone, he whispered, "Words can't express how much I appreciate you and the help you've given me, either."

Heat built inside her, starting down at the very bottoms of her feet, and it swelled quickly to fill her to the brim.

"Thanks," she murmured, not knowing what else to say.

"Jane—" Sloan's voice made her start "—did you know that Greg tested out of high school in the eleventh grade?"

Her eyebrows raised. "Wow." She looked at Greg. "That's impressive."

"Ah—" he waved aside the compliment "—it was nothing."

"His mom had to fight the whole school system to get him the privilege of taking that test," Travis said. He chuckled. "She threatened to sue them."

Jane looked wide-eyed at Greg for confirmation. He laughed.

"That was my mom." His grin got bigger. "She was tiny, but was a barracuda when she had to be. Besides, I had enough credits to graduate. The school board was just being difficult."

"Greg and I have been friends since grade school." Travis spooned out a second helping of sweet-potato casserole. "Sloan is the old man of the group. We didn't meet him until med school."

"Now, now," Sloan said, "let's not start this again." He leveled his gaze on Jane. "Can I be blamed for getting married young and having kids before realizing I wanted to become a doctor?"

"Absolutely not." Jane knew that's the answer Sloan was looking for.

"See there. Jane's on my side." He winked at her. "Smart woman."

And that's the way the day went. Joking, story-telling, laughing. Jane had the time of her life.

"The whole day was perfect, don't you think?"
Jane sipped a glass of wine in front of the hearth.

The fire was burning itself out. But the embers still glowed, hot and inviting. Greg's guests had gone home about thirty minutes ago, and Joy had been asleep for more than an hour. The dishes were washed, the food put away, and all that was left to do was reminisce about the successful gathering.

"It sure was," Greg said. "It's always fun. Our holidays together."

Instinctively, Jane knew he was speaking of his celebration dinners with Travis, Rachel, Sloan and the girls.

"I like your friends. Very much."

But it was evident from the look in his green gaze that Travis, Sloan and the others were not what he wanted to talk about.

"Like I said," he told her, "we always have a good time. But today was extra special. Because of you."

The kiss he'd given her in the kitchen early this morning...the meaningful looks he'd cast her way all day...even his whispered words of appreciation at dinner. All these things had made her feel so... so *special.*

But you shouldn't feel special. The thought floated through her brain like an unwelcome storm cloud. *You can't be special. Not with this ugly lie still planted firmly between you like a hundred-year-old oak tree with branches that reach out and ensnare everyone in its grip.*

Everyone? Jane felt confused. Bewildered as to why that thought would enter her head. She'd only lied to Greg.

Not so. She'd lied to Rachel weeks ago in order

to get an appointment with Greg. And she'd gone along with this dinner, she'd entertained Sloan and Travis and the girls and Rachel…all the while allowing them to believe that her only interest in Greg and Joy was in being the baby's nanny.

All Greg's friends were involved in her lie. They'd become caught up in the tangle of branches that seemed to grow ever more cumbersome, ever more complicated. She had to tell Greg the truth. She just had to tell him before—

Suddenly, his arm was around her shoulder and he was pulling her closer to him.

"The day was perfect," he murmured in a soft and sexy tone, "because you were here to share it with me."

All day long his attention had made her feel so wonderful. But now it made her feel threatened. It was wrong. She couldn't let this go on.

Tell him. Tell him the truth, her conscience scolded her. *Get everything out in the open.*

But the whole day—the whole memory of the day—would be ruined if she blurted out her true identity now. Her wonderful memory would be ruined forever.

Tomorrow, a gentler voice suggested. *Break the news to him gently. Tomorrow.* She latched on to the thought for all she was worth.

"Greg," she said, "I'm awfully tired. It's been a long day."

He looked surprised. He looked hurt. Rebuffed. He took his arm from around her.

"Look, honey," he said, "this isn't what you think. I know you've heard about my…reputation.

But this isn't like that. Not at all. You've got to believe me when I say that you—''

"Wait, Greg. Stop.'' She set her wineglass on the coffee table and stood up. "You've misunderstood me. This has nothing to do with…'' Her voice faded, then she said, "I, um, I'm just really tired right now. Can we talk tomorrow?''

"Sure,'' he said, standing now, too.

He did his best to hide the very obvious rejection he felt, and the confusion swamping him at the abrupt change in her behavior.

Why shouldn't he be confused? She'd encouraged his advances, his tender looks, with silent messages of her own throughout the day. And now here she was shoving him away. Maybe not physically, but with words. With excuses. With more lies.

But the fantasy had gone on for far too long. Greg had become important to her. And she was almost certain she'd become important to him, too. Now both of them would be hurt. Her revelation would bring them both terrible pain.

"But before you slip away from me—''

Immediately, it became abundantly clear that he wasn't yet ready to give up as he reached out to her then, slid his warm, strong fingers over her forearm, and Jane thought for sure she'd melt right where she stood.

"—I need you to know something,'' he continued. "It's important. I want to tell you that I've…well, that I've come to admire you. And not just because you've been such a good nanny for Joy. It's more than that. Much more. It's…personal. Now that I've gotten to know you—'' His thought seemed to stumble and break, haltingly. Finally, he inhaled deeply. "I just want you to know that you've come to mean something to me. Something very important."

Jane's breath left her. She had to think this over, had to tell him the truth—but how?

"We'll talk tomorrow," she said firmly, wanting—*needing*—to get away from him. Now. "I promise." Then she bid him good-night, turned around and left him standing alone by the dying embers.

She'd barely closed her bedroom door when she heard the front doorbell ring.

Chapter Nine

It was obvious to Greg from the moment he opened the front door that Pricilla was a bit tipsy.

Instantly, he found himself shaking his head at the overly diplomatic evaluation. The woman was drunk. His daughter's mother grasped the doorjamb as if the world was tipping off its axis.

"Where is she?" Pricilla demanded, slurring together the last two words of her question. She seemed to want to come into the apartment, but her whole body wavered. In the end, her grip on the door frame tightened and she remained at the threshold.

Greg frowned. "It's after ten. She's right where she should be. In bed."

How could he ever have found this woman attractive? he wondered.

Before this moment, the few memories of the time he'd spent with Pricilla had been hazy. But seeing her in this state helped him to recall the past with more clarity.

Pricilla had been lots of fun to be around at first. She'd been full of humorous stories that had made him laugh. He'd even found her self-centeredness entertaining. During their second date they had slept together. Sleeping with a woman after only two dates wasn't a normal occurrence for Greg. In fact, it was against his dating rules. It was one rule he was sorry he'd broken, for, after that night, things changed. *She'd* changed. Her vainglorious attitude, which he'd found cute and entertaining before, altered to a demanding and temperamental disposition that soon repulsed him. And during their third date, she'd also switched from merely sipping wine to gulping straight liquor. Whisky. No ice.

Alcohol had made Pricilla loud and…coarse, he remembered. And by the end of the evening, Greg had known he wouldn't be interested in seeing her again.

Looking at this woman, he couldn't help but recognize the miracle he'd been blessed with in Jane. Her blue-gray eyes might not be as flashy as Pricilla's, her soft, honey-hued hair might not be as stylish, either, but flash and style were only skin deep. Through Jane, he'd learned that there was much more to a woman's beauty than outside appearance. A lot more. Not that his Jane wasn't beautiful. He dreamed about kissing her luscious lips, roving his fingers over the delicate planes and angles of her lovely face.

Furthermore, he suddenly realized, he'd only been attracted to that shallow sort of flashiness when he'd still been ignorant about what a real relationship with a woman could mean.

And that's what he thought he and Jane had been developing—a *real* relationship. One that, he hoped, would grow into something closer, more intimate. But exploring that would have to wait until tomorrow. Right now, he had to deal with the unexpected appearance of his baby's mother.

Evidently, Pricilla sensed disapproval in his tone, his expression. She paused. And slowly straightened. She took a deep breath. With her free hand, she smoothed back the slight disarray of her elaborately coiffed hair. Tipped up her chin. Moistened her lips, then ran her index finger along the outside rim of her bottom lip as though removing an imaginary smear of lipstick. All of her movements were slow, as though she were moving through air that was viscous and thick.

Then she smiled.

A big smile. Bright. Bold.

"Maybe I should start over," she said, her tone now hovering somewhere between friendly and sultry. "Maybe I should first wish you a happy Thanksgiving."

"Same to you, Pricilla."

Her mouth quirked up at one corner in a saucy grin. "Oh, I've had a very happy day. And it's only going to get happier, I'm sure."

Her voice dropped to a whisper, seemingly meant to make him privy to some sexy secret or other.

"See…I have a gentleman waiting for me out in the parking lot. He drove me into the city in his candy-apple-red Beamer. Luscious car." Her tongue darted out to touch the apex of her top lip. "Luscious man."

Greg knew the root cause of Pricilla's absurd behavior was the abundance of alcohol she'd obviously consumed before arriving on his doorstep, but that didn't stop him from finding her conduct rude and intrusive. She had no right showing up at his home demanding to see her daughter when she was in such a state.

"And as soon as I get a chance to talk to her," she continued, "I plan to focus all my attention on that luscious man waiting down there for me." Her delicately arched brows waggled suggestively.

Obviously, she wanted Greg to feel as if he would be missing out on something most exciting. But all he felt was disdain. And pity.

He guessed he should have expected her appearance. It was a holiday. Wasn't it normal for any mother to want to see her child on Thanksgiving? Even a mother as seemingly unthinking enough to show up for a visit past a child's bedtime, not to mention showing up in her intoxicated condition.

That thought gave rise to yet another: would the woman be appearing, drunk and on the verge of disorderly, on every special occasion? There were so many of them: Christmas, New Year's, Joy's birthday, Valentine's Day…at this instant, the list of yearly celebrations seemed endless to him.

He couldn't help but think he would be setting a precedent for years to come in his reaction to Pricilla tonight. Should he be kind and welcoming, forgiving the fact that she looked and smelled as if she'd fallen into a vat of one-hundred-proof vodka? Or should he

put his foot down right now? Let her know in no
uncertain terms that his home was not to be used for
her drunken theatrics? That she should not show up
here again unless she called first? And even then,
only if she was clearheaded?

But who was he to tell Pricilla that she couldn't
see her daughter on holidays? Or any other day, for
that matter? Would he like being kept away from his
baby girl?

A surprising sea of sorrow washed over him at the
mere thought. No grinning gurgles. No wet, smack-
ing kisses. No pats on the cheek. No sleepy sighs.
No tiny face pressed against his shoulder in slumber.

He actually gave his head a tiny shake back and
forth. He couldn't imagine a day going by without
seeing Joy, without loving her, without experiencing
life through her innocent eyes. He may have only
had her in his home for a month, but he couldn't
conceive of life without her. Such an existence
would be empty. Worthless.

So with those thoughts running through his head,
he couldn't bring himself to tell Pricilla not to come
to his home, not to visit her daughter.

But above all else, a stern, paternal voice echoed
in his brain, loud, adamant, refusing to be ignored,
Joy must be protected.

He had no idea where the voice had come from,
and upon hearing it he actually gave a jerky start and
blinked. He hadn't even realized he'd become so
sheltering of his baby girl.

It was then that he was walloped with a realization. It seemed that somewhere along the road he'd
become a father. A real, honest-to-goodness daddy

who only wanted what was best for his daughter. To hell with what might be best for anyone else. And that included his little girl's mother.

At that moment, Pricilla looked over his shoulder and made a move to enter his home. A protective instinct reared up inside Greg, the likes of which he'd never before experienced. He stepped in front of her, blocking her access.

"Look, Pricilla," he said, leveling a gaze at her dead square in the eyes, "I think what you should do is turn around and go on down there to your friend. You can come back tomorrow. When you're sober. You'll be welcome then."

Her pretty blue eyes narrowed the slightest bit and her chin tucked down defensively.

"Well, what you think and what I think are two different things, now, aren't they?" she said softly, challenge clear and unmistakable. "I'm coming in to see her. I know she's here. I have a few things I want to say. Then I'll be on my way." Again, she repeated, "I *know* she's here."

Her words seemed to make no sense. "I'm not disputing that. Of course, Joy is here. You left her here with me, remember?"

Impatience marred the woman's features with sharp angles and deep furrows. "I'm not talking about *the kid*—"

"Wait!"

Jane's sharp tone propelled Greg into a one-hundred-and-eighty-degree pivot. The panic written on Jane's face made his heart hitch in his chest. She was obviously afraid of the inebriated stranger who had shown up at the front door in the dead of night.

Meaning to reassure her, he lifted his hand, palm out…but then he noticed she wasn't looking at him. Her attention was focused on Pricilla.

"Don't!" Jane said. "Please, don't do this. He doesn't know."

Greg frowned. Doesn't know? Doesn't know what? What was she talking about?

His confusion was so thorough, his vigilant guard lowered. He was no longer blocking the door as securely as he had been and Pricilla pushed her way past him.

"I'm talking about *her*," Pricilla said, pointing in Jane's direction, continuing to address Greg. "My *push*y—" she shoved her finger toward Jane on the emphasized syllable of each forcefully and expressively spoken word "—*over*bearing, *dom*ineering *sis*ter."

Time seemed to slow to half speed for Greg. Surreal. *Un*real. A dream. A *nightmare*.

Words and thoughts floated in and out of his mind, incomplete and out-of-joint, as he stared in total disbelief at the two women facing off in his living room.

"You are a real piece of work."

Pricilla plunked her lacquered-nailed hands on her hips as she spoke. The blood-red polish on her fingertips stood out against the cream-colored silk she wore. Strange, Greg thought, for him to notice the stark contrast of color at a time like this. When he should be asking questions. Getting to the bottom of this disconcerting mess.

"You move out of our apartment," Pricilla continued to rant at Jane, "leaving no forwarding address. How rude you are. I'd still be looking for you if Max hadn't been working today.''

Max. Greg wondered why that name should sound so familiar to him. The answer seemed to hover, fuzzy, just out of reach at the edges of his brain.

"You walked out on your job," the blonde accused Jane. She wobbled slightly on her high-heeled shoes. "You left Max in an awful lurch."

Finally, Jane spoke. "I left to look for you. And Joy. I waited for a week, Pricilla. I *agonized* for a week, not knowing where you'd taken the baby—"

"She's my baby," Pricilla interrupted viciously.

Greg watched as one strand of her hair, the very strand she'd pushed back at the door, now fell into her eyes unheeded.

"She was *my* baby to do with as *I* pleased." A derisive, snorting sound erupted from Pricilla. "The little runt nearly ruined my life. *You* nearly ruined my life, Jane. Dirty diapers and canned formula and crying babies. Dumping that kid here was the best thing I ever did for myself."

Quietly, Jane said, "Well, we both know you're good at that."

Pricilla glared at Jane.

"You always do what's best for you. You always have. Regardless of the needs or wants of anyone else."

"Who better to watch out for than yourself?"

Greg saw sadness creep over Jane's delicate features, and then after a moment she said, "Mother's famous last words."

The blonde tossed out another bold and overly bright smile. "I learned from the best."

This statement only seemed to exacerbate Jane's disappointment.

"I had hoped," Jane said, "that over the years you'd have learned a little something from me."

"Oh, yes." Pricilla's eyes went wide, her tone becoming, melodramatic. "Let's learn from Ms. Sacrifice herself. Let's drop out of college. Let's get a job that has long hours and low pay. Let's survive as one big, happy family."

"We were a happy family." Jane worried the back of one thumb with the pad of the other, her agitation apparent. "And we were surviving just fine."

"*You* might have been happy," Pricilla charged, "but I have never been one to tolerate merely surviving. I need fun. I need abundance. I need money."

"You need men."

Pricilla grinned. "Them, too."

Joy's mother seemed unhurt by the sting Jane had thrown. Greg knew he should step in, that he should break up this conversation before it escalated into something really ugly. He could clearly see that's where this was headed. But he was still too shocked to speak.

Jane knew Pricilla. *But could she really be Pricilla's sister?* The notion was mind-boggling, and he was sure that all the implications of this bombshell still hadn't revealed themselves to him.

The lies Jane had told him flitted and danced around in his mind.

But he didn't feel angry. All he felt was…oddly detached.

"I can see you're disappointed in me, dear sister,"

Pricilla said. "Don't you think I've always known that you find me one big disappointment?"

Her tone took on the quality of a purring cat as she continued, "Why is it, Jane, that you never figured out why you couldn't get me to conform to your rules and regulations, to your high moral standards?"

The room was still as Pricilla's taunting question hung heavy in the air.

Pricilla said, "Let me answer that for you." Her brow furrowed with an ugly frown. "Because I never cared what you thought or how you felt about me. That's why. I wanted what I wanted. And I was— and still am—determined to get it. Any way I can."

"I provided for you," Jane quietly pointed out.

"You didn't provide enough." Pricilla reached up and shoved the lock of hair from her face. "It takes time and energy to get what I want from the men I date. I just can't be saddled with a kid. Why could you never understand that?"

"Well then, why didn't you just leave Joy with me?"

It was the first time Jane had raised her voice. Automatically, Greg found himself inching toward her, guided by some strange need…some mysterious urge. Her eyes welled with tears, and her face crumpled with emotion. He stopped several feet from her, an invisible, impenetrable wall seeming to separate them.

"You could have packed up your things and left if that's what you wanted to do," Jane spat out. "If things were so bad for you, you could have run away with the first man who would have you. But you shouldn't have taken that baby away from me. It was torture! Sheer torture!''

Jane sniffed, and in an obvious attempt to regain some of her dignity, she swiped at her tears with the back of one hand.

Despite the lies she'd told him, despite everything, Greg wanted to go to her, wanted to comfort her, but for some reason he didn't. He couldn't. So he simply stood, silent, rooted to the spot.

"You want to know why I took Joy?"

Pricilla seemed unaffected by Jane's tearful diatribe.

"I took the kid away because I was mad at you. I was mad as hell that you manipulated me. You made me feel guilty. If it wasn't for all the guilt you laid on my shoulders, I'd have never given birth to the kid. I'd have been as free as a bluebird in the treetops." She switched her weight to the other hip. "But you forced me to endure that god-awful pregnancy—I'll never forgive you for those horrible months I spent fat and miserable. I'll never forget the awful pain of having that kid come out of me. And as if that hadn't been enough, you then made me feel guilty about wanting to go out and have a little fun. 'You're a mother now,' you said. 'You have to stop partying and carousing,' you said.''

Pricilla made a mockery of Jane with a squeaky, unflattering, holier-than-thou imitation.

"But I am free," the woman continued, unrelenting. "I'm free of you. And I'm free of the kid. And leaving the both of you behind is—"

"The best thing you ever did," Jane quietly concluded. "Yes, you've already said that.''

Silence seemed to echo off the living room walls. Then Pricilla glanced at Greg. She giggled suddenly, her eyes registering surprise.

"I'd forgotten you were here," she told him. She heaved a sigh, and smoothed her palms down her silk-clad thighs. She looked at Jane again. "My, but I feel better. I went to the apartment today to tell you all this, but you weren't there. When I went to the restaurant, Max told me you'd gotten a job with some doctor in Philadelphia." Her cackle of laughter was sharp. "I about split my gut when I heard that. 'There she goes again,' I told myself, 'manipulating her way into people's lives.'" Her blond head tilted to one side, her eyes taking on a wounded look. "I know you always cared more about the kid than you did about me."

"Oh, Pricilla, that's not true."

"It is! And you and I both know why, too."

Greg's gaze cut sharply to Jane, who had pressed her lips together, guilt seeming to ooze off her in thick sheets. The whole scene was growing stranger by the moment.

Jane began, "Look—"

"No." Pricilla cut her off by swiping her hand through the air. "I've said what I came to say. I'm ready to go. I have someone waiting for me." Then she turned to Greg. "I also came to warn you about Jane. She's manipulative. And she's not above using guilt to get people to do exactly what she wants." Squaring her shoulders and tipping up her chin, she admitted, "I lied about you. I'm sure she's tattled on me. Revealed all the lies I told her about how you refused to help me with the kid." Her mouth quirked up at one corner. "I'd like to say I'm sorry, but I really can't. I was watching out for myself. It's a tough job, but somebody's gotta do it."

Without another word and only the slightest of wobbles, Pricilla sauntered to the door. It took two tries for her to get it open, but then she was gone.

The dull ache swelling in Jane's chest felt like it was surely going to suffocate her. She knew what it was. She'd lived with this dreadful feeling every single day since moving in with Greg and Joy.

It was fear.

Fear of being discovered.

But now the pain had grown. Metamorphosed into something new. Something gargantuan.

This unbearable lead balloon inflating inside her was the fear of Greg's reaction now that he had discovered the truth about her identity.

Of course, he'd had to find out. However, this wasn't how she meant for it to happen.

Her eyes darted to Greg. He stood there, seemingly frozen in place as he stared at the closed front door. His handsome features were devoid of emotion. But Jane knew that was only due to the shock he'd received. Soon the awful truth would sink in, his mind would assimilate all the information he'd learned from Pricilla's visit. Then his muscles would thaw. And his feelings of anger and betrayal would soon be bubbling to the surface like molten lava.

Her fear warned her—urged her—to run. To flee before he had the chance to react. She realized that was only her natural-born instinct of fight or flight…and she didn't believe she had any more fight left in her.

But running would be wrong. She'd told Greg stories. She'd lived under his roof allowing him to believe half truths and lies about who she was, where she'd come from, and she'd hidden from him her relationship with Joy.

"So that was the sister—"

The melting process had begun, and Jane felt her mouth go dry at the sound of Greg's cold tone.

"—from whom I was waiting for a call."

Jane didn't answer. It was clear he wasn't asking a question. So she only remained silent and stood there.

"That was the person who was going to give you a great reference. Pricilla was the person for whom you baby-sat. Joy was the baby you helped raise."

He was putting the story together quickly. Guilt weighed so heavily on her, she could hardly keep eye contact with him. But she forced herself to hold her head up, her gaze level with his. Knowing what he was going through, the shock of the truth he was just now discovering, Jane felt he deserved an eye-to-eye connection.

"Lies," he said. "It was all a bunch of lies. I can't even count all the lies you told me."

"They weren't all lies, Greg," she said quietly. "You've got to believe me."

"Why? Why do I have to believe you? Why should I believe anything that comes out of your mouth?"

He was hurting. Oh, my, how he was hurting. She

could clearly see that. His green eyes were hazed over with the pain he was experiencing.

"Please…" She'd never felt the need to plead so urgently as she did at this moment. "Please, Greg, let me explain."

A war was being waged inside him. That was clear. Would he agree to listen to her story? Or would he walk away from her? Jane knew she'd have to live with the winner of the battle, knew she'd be forced to be content with whatever decision he ultimately came to.

It felt as though many long moments passed, even though she knew no more than ten seconds could have ticked away. Finally, he moved. He walked over to the couch and sat down.

"I'm listening." Then he crossed his arms tightly over his chest and waited.

Hesitantly, she went and sat down in the chair adjacent to the couch. With nervous fingers, she reached up and absently scratched her chin, tucked a strand of hair behind her ear, worried her earlobe, all the while pondering where to start her explanation.

"When I came to your office for the first time," she began, "it wasn't with the intention of lying about who I was. I came there—" Apprehension had her feeling the need to pause and swallow. "I came to you intending to ask you if you had seen Pricilla and Joy. You see, they had been gone a week. And I had no idea where they were."

The agony and worry she had endured during that awful, lonely week made her eyes grow misty.

Inhaling a shaky breath, she continued, "B-but, if

you think back, you'll remember that you were late. I sat there in that examining room for a long time. Just thinking. Worrying. And wondering.''

He gave a light nod, and Jane knew he remembered the day and the fact that he had been running late.

"I hadn't wanted to come see you at all," Jane admitted. "Back when Pricilla first told me she was pregnant, I advised her to contact you. To give you the opportunity to offer her some help." She licked her lips and acknowledged, "Monetary help. You see, we needed it. Pricilla wasn't working. Hadn't ever worked, really. And on my wages as a waitress..."

She shook her head. "I'm not staying on track very well, am I? Anyway, Pricilla told me that she'd talked with you, and that you...weren't very nice about the idea of a baby. That you refused to give any help at all unless you were given total custody. Pricilla suggested we agree, that we give you Joy, but—" again, Jane was forced to swallow "—but I just couldn't let that happen."

Jane didn't feel the need to go into just how deeply she was against that idea, or why.

"She never came to me."

His chilly tone frightened Jane. This wasn't going well at all.

"I know that. I do know that. Now. But I didn't know it then. While I was waiting to see you in your office that first day, I was frantic. And not thinking clearly. I had looked for Pricilla and Joy everywhere. I'd called and visited all her friends. No one had a clue where they might be. S-so in desperation, I ended up in your office.''

She rubbed her fingertips back and forth across her lips. ''But at the last minute, I realized I might be making a mistake. I thought you might frown on the idea of Pricilla disappearing with Joy like that, with no job and no money, a-and that you might make some trouble for us. See a lawyer. Try to take Joy from us—from Pricilla, I mean.

''And just as I was about ready to leave the office, you arrived.'' She moistened her dry lips. ''So...I lied. About who I was and why I was there. And I'm sorry.''

Disapproval dulled his gaze.

''Please try to understand,'' she pleaded. ''I practically raised that baby for ten months. I love Joy. Like she was my own.''

Guilt rolled over her, and she hoped he didn't suspect the full truth behind her desperation where Joy was concerned.

''I hadn't seen hide nor hair of Joy for a week. I was in a panic. I was sick with worry. And when you said you had a little girl, my thoughts just went into total chaos. When you offered me a job as Joy's nanny, I thought I'd died and gone straight to heaven.''

Hot tears scalded her eyes, but she refused to let them fall. ''I wanted to see her so badly. I wanted to be with her.'' She dashed away the single teardrop from high on her cheek. ''So I let you believe that I was just a woman who was unemployed and down on her luck and in need of a job and a place to stay.''

Sucking in a quiet breath, she continued, ''I

quickly learned you're nothing like the man my sister described you to be. I can't believe how I've come to care about you. How I've come to—''

Careful, her brain hastened to warn. Now wasn't the time to reveal her heart. In fact, at this moment Jane truly believed there would never be a time that she could reveal the full extent of her feelings for this man.

"The only thing I'm guilty of," she said, "is not revealing to you that I'm Pricilla's sister and Joy's aunt. Everything else I ever said to you was the truth. The honest truth."

He sat there, and Jane easily imagined him to be a powerful judge weighing the fate of her future.

She could hold back the all-important question no longer. "Are you going to kick me out, Greg? Are you going to keep Joy away from me? Please, I'm begging you. Please allow me to have some small part in that baby's life. Please. I understand if you're angry. If you're disappointed and disillusioned. And feeling betrayed. You have the right to feel all of those things. And every bit of that is my fault. But, please…''

Her voice trailed into oblivion when he shook his head and stood up.

"I don't know," he said. "I don't know what to think."

Then he walked out of the room, leaving her sitting there all alone.

Chapter Ten

"I should have put two and two together weeks ago." Greg paced the small conference room, making circles around the table where Sloan sat.

"But we're in the medical profession, Greg," his friend pointed out. "Two and two rarely if ever equal a concrete answer. There are too many variant factors."

But Greg barely heard him. "How could she do this?"

Just then Travis shouldered his way into the room balancing three foam cups. "Got here as quick as I could. Stopped off for decaf coffee. So, Greg, which patient is in crisis? And what happened?" He looked down at the empty conference table. "Where are the patient's files?"

Emergency meetings were rare in their practice. And before tonight, the gatherings had always been called to discuss a specific patient's imminent distress. However, after having lain awake nearly two hours, emotions eating a damned hole in his stomach, Greg had called this meeting to address his own crisis.

He needed advice. He needed strong shoulders to lean on. He needed friends on whom he could safely vent. He'd called Sloan and Travis.

"It's not a patient." Sloan reached for his cup of coffee and popped off the lid.

"It's Jane," Greg said, raking his fingers through his hair.

Travis looked confused. "But we just left your place a couple hours ago. Everything was fine."

Sloan inhaled steam rising from the coffee. "Seems Joy's mother showed up after everyone left."

Again, Travis's dark brows gathered as he evidently searched his brain for some information. "What was her name? Patsy?"

"Pricilla," Greg supplied.

"Yes. I remember now." Travis smiled. "Well, isn't that nice? Joy's mother coming to visit on Thanksgiving."

"From Greg's description," Sloan said, "it wasn't so nice. The woman had been drinking."

Greg corrected him, "The woman was sloshed out of her gourd."

Travis whistled. "Did you let her see the baby?"

Dark, heavy thoughts weighed on Greg's mind. "She didn't come to see Joy. She came to see her *sister*."

Travis just shook his head. "I'd better sit down. I have no clue what's going on here."

Quietly, Sloan explained, "Jane is Pricilla's sister."

Finally realizing just how tangled the ensnaring web of the situation was, Travis gave another low whistle. "Jane is Joy's aunt. That means Jane lied—"

Sloan cut him off with a sharp look. Evidently, Greg's friends didn't want him getting any more upset than he already was. But it was too late. Greg didn't think he could get any more upset than he was right at this moment.

"As I sat on the edge of my mattress tonight," Greg said, "things came to me. Things I should have thought of weeks ago. You know, Jane's story was off. The story she gave me that very first day back there in the examining room. She said she needed a physical for a job—*a job she hadn't even lined up yet*. That's not the normal sequence of events. A person gets a job first, they obtain physical forms from their new place of employment, and then they see a doctor. Not the other way around. Why didn't I realize then that this was all a sham? I fell for her ploy, hook, line and sinker. She said she needed a job, and I opened up my home, my family, opened up my whole life to her."

"Stop being so hard on yourself," Travis said.

"You had a need of your own. A big need." Sloan planted his elbows on the tabletop, then laced his fingers together. "You needed help with Joy. Badly, if you'll remember correctly. Maybe it was that need that kept you blind and deaf to anything else but what you saw as the solution to your problem."

Greg sighed. "That makes me sound pretty lame."

"It makes you sound human," Travis said.

The room was silent for a moment.

Then Greg said, "You know, she had a good reason behind the lie she told."

Both his friends looked interested.

"Pricilla had lied to Jane about me," he told them. "Jane thought of me as some sort of big, bad wolf. She'd been led to believe that I wanted no part of Joy's life unless I was given full custody. That I'd refused to help Pricilla and Joy with monetary or emotional support."

He explained Jane's position until a deeper understanding shone in both the men's gazes.

"However," Greg finally said, "even though she had what she felt was a good motivation, that doesn't change the fact that she lied. And she continued the ruse, continued to keep me in the dark regarding her real identity, even after she found out that all the things Pricilla had said about me weren't true."

"She was probably scared to tell you the truth," Sloan offered, "after she'd let it go on for so long."

"She let it go on for so long," Travis repeated his friend's words, "that her feelings for you changed. They deepened. Developed into something much more intense than she expected. I saw it when we were all together for Thanksgiving."

Sloan nodded. "And your feelings for her have developed into something pretty amazing, too. Don't try to deny it, Greg. You know it's true."

Greg remained silent. Sloan was right. He couldn't deny it.

"I've never seen you happier," Sloan quietly continued. "Yes, part of that happiness is due to Joy's arrival in your life. But it's more than that. It's Jane. She makes you feel good. Needed. She makes you feel…content. I've never seen you more settled, more satisfied than since you met Jane. She changed your life. You have to admit that."

It was true, Greg realized. So very true.

"So it's understandable that she couldn't bring herself to reveal the truth," Travis added. "The relationship you two shared was changing, growing, every single day." He shrugged. "Not to mention her maternal-feelings for the baby."

Something Pricilla had said to Jane came to Greg.

If it wasn't for all the guilt you laid on my shoulders, I'd have never given birth to the kid.

"Oh, heaven help me," he groaned.

Pricilla would have aborted his daughter! If it hadn't been for Jane, Greg would never have experienced the delight of being Joy's father.

"What?" Sloan asked.

"Nothing," he said, feeling this topic too intimate to share with even his best friends.

"So, what are you going to do?" Travis asked him.

Greg simply shook his head as he tried to push aside the huge realization and focus on how he felt about what Jane had done. He exhaled. "It's funny, but it's not really anger I'm feeling. I'm hurt. I feel almost wounded by the fact that she lied. That she didn't feel I could handle the truth. That she couldn't come to me with her problem. Explain things to me."

"But how could she do that when you and your reaction *was* the problem?" Sloan asked. Without waiting for an answer, he said, "Are you going to allow her to continue watching Joy?"

Then Travis asked, "Can she be trusted?"

White-hot anger rolled over Greg, seemingly out of nowhere.

"Of course she can be trusted!"

Why? Greg wondered. Why was he taking up for Jane now after he'd just discovered that she'd lied her way into his home, into his and his daughter's lives?

"Because I can feel it," he said, answering his own unspoken questions. "Here." Curling his fingers into his palm, he pressed his balled fist against his solar plexus. "In my gut, I know I can trust her. I've never met a woman like Jane. She's extraordinary. Remarkable, really. She's passionate about her beliefs. She's confident. Poised. Self-reliant. And she has been for a long time. She's giving." He thought of Jane's adolescence. How she quit school to get a job in order to provide for her sister. "Sometimes to a fault. She's proved she can handle tough situations. And she's the smartest person I've ever met. Not book smart, maybe, but *people* smart. *Life* smart."

"My Lord, look at the man," Travis breathed. "He's lit up like a light bulb."

Sloan nodded. "Looks like love to me."

Overwhelming elation had Greg making for the door. Sloan was right. Over his shoulder, he called, "I'm wasting my breath telling you guys all this. I'm going home. And tomorrow, Jane and I are going to talk."

* * *

The next morning, Jane got herself dressed and then began packing her bags. She had slept fitfully, waking time and again from bad dreams. In each and every nightmare, Joy was being torn from her arms.

Jane had no idea how she was going to survive living away from Joy. But after seeing Pricilla last night, after hearing all the hateful things her sister had to say, after finally realizing what kind of person Pricilla had turned out to be, Jane couldn't help but come to the sad conclusion that she didn't deserve—

A soft knock on the bedroom door had her whirling around.

"Jane, can I come in?"

Panic welled in her chest at the sound of Greg's voice. She had known she'd have to face him this morning. But she wasn't ready yet.

Would she ever be ready? she wondered.

"I'd like to talk," he said when she didn't answer.

Reluctance coated her tone as if it were a tangible thing as she said, "Come in."

He looked tired. It was quite obvious that he'd experienced the same kind of restless night as she.

"What are you doing?"

The touch of alarm that tinged his question made her frown.

"I—I'm packing," she said. "I was sure that you'd—"

"But we haven't even had a chance to talk."

Absently, she smoothed her palm against the cotton fabric of the blouse she'd been folding. Her arms relaxed and she dropped the blouse on the bed. She watched him pace over to the window and look out at the chilly November morning.

He turned to face her, his green eyes grave, his expression utterly serious.

"Look, Jane," he said, "I'm not happy that you lied. But I do understand how this whole mess started." He stepped over to the chest of drawers and reached out to unwittingly fiddle with the brass pull. "Of course, I wish you had told me the truth weeks ago."

She averted her gaze and whispered, "I wish I had, too."

"But Sloan helped me to see—"

"Sloan? You've talked about this with your friends?"

He nodded. "I called both Sloan and Travis last night. We met at the office."

"I did hear you go out," she admitted. "But I thought you might have been needed at the hospital."

He just shook his head. "I needed to talk. To work this out in my mind."

Knowing that Greg's friends knew the truth, that she'd lied, Jane was terribly embarrassed. But they'd have found out sooner or later, anyway. She was just glad that Greg had good friends who would be there for him in good times...and in bad times.

That was more than she had.

"The guys helped me to see," he repeated, "that you must have been too afraid to tell me."

With her gaze riveted to the floor, she couldn't stop the small, sad smile that formed on her mouth.

Apparently, his friends understood what she'd been feeling.

"I was, Greg," she told him. "I was very afraid of how you'd react."

"I'd have understood. I'd have listened to your story. I—I'd have…"

His words petered out, and she lifted her chin to look at him.

Would you have? Really? she silently asked.

His eyelids closed and he groaned softly. As if he'd heard her unasked question, he admitted, "Oh, Jane. I hope I would have. But I can't say for sure how I would have reacted. I just can't say."

When he looked at her again, his green gaze glittered with hope, with a positive energy that had Jane's stomach twisting in knots of confusion. His admission made her believe he understood her motive. She felt less guilty.

She'd be leaving on more equal ground than she'd arrived.

"I came in here to ask if we could just put this all behind us," he said. "I want us to start building a trusting relationship. Right now. From this moment on, there will be no secrets between us."

A trusting relationship?

What was it he was looking for? Did he want them to form a relationship for Joy's sake? Or was he asking for something more personal? More intimate?

The questions frightened her. And excited her at the same time.

However, she couldn't allow herself to contemplate any kind of relationship with Greg. And she had more than one reason why she couldn't.

"Greg—" His name issued from her throat in a dry, raspy sound. She swallowed and tried again. "Greg, I'm leaving. This morning."

"But didn't you just hear what I said?" he asked. "I don't want you to leave."

"This has nothing to do with what you want," she quietly said. "Or what I want. I *have* to leave. I can't be a part of Joy's life."

"What are you talking about?"

"I thought this through last night. Joy deserves to be raised by someone who can do a good job. She needs love and discipline and guidance. She needs a parent who's going to help her grow into a good and decent person. I'm not her parent. I don't have what it takes to see that she grows up to be a proper young woman."

"Jane, you're confusing me." He reached up and touched his chin. "What you're saying makes no sense. You love Joy. Love her so very much. All that you've done, the lies you told, were all so that you could be with Joy."

Emotion welled up in her throat, threatening to choke off all speech, and hot tears burned the backs of her eyelids. She sank down onto the edge of the bed.

"Oh, Greg." She felt utterly miserable. "I tried so hard to raise Pricilla right. Our mother was a horrible role model. She had men in and out of the house. She used people to get what she wanted rather than work for an honest wage. I did everything I could to see that Pricilla had everything she should need." Jane felt a tear roll down her face and plop on the back of her hand. "But as Pricilla herself said,

I never provided enough. I didn't work hard enough. It's so obvious that I wasn't a good example for my sister. I don't want Joy to suffer just because I'm terrible at raising children. I love her too much—''

"Jane. Oh, Jane."

Besides all that, her brain roared seemingly out of nowhere, *I can't stay here because I've fallen so deeply and passionately in love with you that I'd never survive the disappointed look I'd see in your eyes were you ever to discover the whole truth about me.* She couldn't let that happen. She didn't want to face Greg's disillusionment or his rejection if he was to find out just how worthless she was as a woman.

He'd told her he admired her. He'd just said he didn't want her to leave. Knowing these things would have to be comfort enough as she grew old all alone.

His weight made the mattress dip as he sat down next to her. He took her hand and smoothed her skin with the pad of his thumb.

"You did the best you could do, honey."

Hearing the sweet nickname only made Jane's chin tremble with emotion.

"When you told me the story of your past, I got the impression that your sister—that Pricilla—was nearly grown when your mom left. She was a teenager. You were in your first year of college."

Jane could only nod.

"Your mother had lots of years to influence Pricilla," he continued softly. "Who knows? Maybe your sister inherited your mother's genes. Maybe she'd have ended up with the same self-centered attitude even if she'd been born with perfect parents. No one can say for certain.''

''But I tried so hard to make sure that she didn't turn out like Mother.''

His arm slid around her shoulders like a warm, protective coat. ''Maybe you did make a few mistakes. You were young yourself, remember. A teen raising a teen, really. In trying to give her everything, in working hard so that she wouldn't have to, maybe what you taught her was that she didn't have to pitch in. She didn't have to take responsibility for herself. In making her the most important thing in the world to you, maybe you made her believe she should be the most important thing in the world to everyone. Especially to herself. At least, that's the Pricilla I came to know in the short time she and I were together.''

Guilt hit Jane like a brick wall. ''So it *is* all my fault.''

''No, honey—''

There it was again. That velvet-sweet name.

''—it isn't your fault at all. There comes a time when each of us needs to become accountable for our own actions. Pricilla's a full-grown woman now. She has been for quite some time. She's responsible for the things she says and does. No one has to answer for her actions but her.''

It felt good having him close, having his warm, silken voice calming her, reassuring her. The urge to lean into him was strong. To let him be her tower of strength. To rest her head on his shoulder and surrender to the heat that skittered and danced in her belly. If only for a moment.

She stiffened. And then leaned away from him so that his arm was forced from her shoulder. She couldn't stay, not for another moment. If she did, she'd surrender to the urge to reveal her heart—as well as her medical condition.

"I have to go." She couldn't look him in the eye. "I have no talent for raising children. Joy deserves better than what I can give her."

"Oh, that's just plain silly, Jane."

His sloughing off of her statement felt as if he'd taken a knife and jabbed her right in the heart. That's how bad his scoffing comment hurt.

"You love Joy," he said. "And Joy loves you. You want what's best for her. Do you think any parent has more than that when they're raising their kids?"

She looked at the floor, worrying her bottom lip between her teeth.

"Besides—"

He gently took her chin between his fingers and thumb and forced her to look him in the eye.

"—I need you to be here. I need your help. I want you. Here."

His gaze intensified as he added, "I love you, Jane."

Her eyes widened. Oh, no. Oh, no. She'd never expected this. Yes, he'd said he admired her but...

"I owe you so much," he said. "I want you to know that I do understand all that you've done."

Confusion knit Jane's brows.

"I know that without your efforts—" his tone dropped to a mere whisper "—Joy might never have been born. I heard what Pricilla said. She'd have aborted my daughter. I'm so very grateful.''

Greg picked up her hand and kissed the back of it, his lips warm and firm.

"But gratitude isn't all I feel," he continued. "Your actions, what you did for Joy, that's all a part of Jane—the woman I love. I love you because you make me feel like I've never felt before. You're strong. I'm in awe of that fact. And you make me feel strong, too. Like I could solve any problem. Like I could take on the world and win. I want you with me. Forever.''

Again, he kissed her hand. The tips of her fingers.

"I don't know what the future may bring," he said. "Who knows if Pricilla won't one day straighten out her life? That she might want custody of Joy?''

Jane inadvertently gasped at the idea.

Greg hugged her hand to his chest. "I wouldn't like it and I'd fight it, tooth and nail, but I could handle it. As long as you were by my side. I want you to marry me, Jane. Say you'll be my wife.''

"Oh, please don't ask that of me. Please. Please, don't, Greg.''

She'd wounded him. She could tell. She felt horrible. This had all gone too far. She'd have to tell him everything now. She'd have to expose herself. There would be no escape.

"I don't mean to hurt you," she said. "You have to believe me. But, Greg…I don't want you to love me. You'll only get hurt. Trust me.''

Bewilderment shadowed his handsome face.

"There are things you don't know about me," she

continued. "In some ways, I'm just as selfish as Pricilla. I did make her feel guilty. I did do everything in my power to persuade her keep her baby. I was so sure she'd have regretted having an abortion. Maybe not right away, but someday…"

Her voice trailed, and she had to wonder, given the mean-spirited side of Pricilla she'd seen last night, if she still felt that her sister would regret such an action. Jane honestly couldn't say.

"But there was another reason I did all I could to convince Pricilla to give birth to Joy."

Her exhalation was shaky. She wasn't proud of her actions. No, she wasn't. How could she make him understand?

"I was so happy, so filled with utter joy, when Pricilla told me she was pregnant. And when the baby was born, my joy seemed to know no limits. Of course, Pricilla was less than pleased. She was sullen and angry, but she was glad to have the pregnancy over with. That poor baby was two days old, and still Pricilla refused to come up with a name. So I named her. My Joy." Jane's mouth spread with a smile. "I was so happy."

It was time for the whole truth. There could be no avoiding it. Not now. Not after Greg had revealed his love for her. Or who he thought she was.

"You see, Greg," she said, keeping her tone as brave as possible, "I can't have children." She told herself to ignore the way his eyes widened in surprise. "Remember the accident I told you about? The car that hit me? Well, I was released from the hospital before the doctors realized that my cervix had been damaged. A tiny tear was all it was. But it was enough to cause an infection. The tear and the infection led to scarring. I'll never conceive a child. I'll never experience the wonder of giving birth. I can't give you a family.'' She averted her gaze and murmured, ''I'm sure you'd be sorry you fell in love with me.''

She forced herself to look at him. ''So, you see, I am just as selfish and self-centered as my sister. I wanted Pricilla to have that baby so I'd have a child in my life. I was certain that my sister would come to love her daughter. In time. But she never did. And it looks as if she never will.''

Jane pulled her hand from his grasp. ''You made me feel beautiful. You made me feel sensual.'' Emotion knotted in her throat. ''I care about you more than you'll ever know.'' She hesitated, and then revealed, ''I love you. But I can't be with you. It wouldn't be fair to you. I can't give you what a normal woman could. A family of your own.''

''Oh, Jane.'' He reached for her. Tugged her into his arms, emotion turning his voice thick. ''Can't you understand,'' he whispered against her ear, ''you are my family. I feel closer to you than anyone else in the world. You have my heart. And my soul. You've become my whole life. You had me from the very first day we met. This was meant to be. I can feel it. Can't you?''

She felt a delicious chuckle rumble deep in his throat.

''You should have learned, seeing the rag-tag family that Sloan and Travis and I have tried to form, that blood relations aren't as important as…well, as *love* relations.''

He pulled back far enough to look deeply into her eyes, and the expression she saw there thrilled her to the very marrow of her bones.

"But...are you sure—"

"Shhh." He lovingly pressed his index finger against her lips. "It's *you* I love, honey. It's *you* I want to spend my life with."

He didn't see her as the empty vessel she'd imagined he might—that she'd imagined herself to be all these years. In fact, her own poor self image had probably been her worst enemy all along.

Jane felt literally walloped with the revelation. "Why didn't I see it before?" she asked, more of herself than him. "I worked so hard to love my mother and my sister, yet neither of them responded to me at all. It's pretty obvious that I was offering my love to the wrong people."

It might have been a hard lesson, but the hard ones were always the best ones, weren't they? Hard lessons were the ones that stuck with you for life.

She looked into Greg's eyes, then, and all she witnessed was a man gazing at—passionately desiring—the woman he loved. A woman he respected. A woman he cherished. She'd never felt more whole than she did at this point in her life.

Another lesson learned: there *was* a man who could make her feel loved. There *was* a soul mate who would love her for her...and not be concerned for what she could not give him. There was a man who could offer her pure, unadulterated love.

And that man was Greg.

Light-hearted laughter erupted from her throat. She felt as if a great weight had been suddenly lifted off her shoulders. He had no idea she was learning and growing in these moments as she was being cradled in his secure embrace. She'd never felt such happiness.

He smiled, love shining bright in his gaze, and Jane felt her world grow as warm as sunshine. Laughter bubbled from her throat.

"You going to let me in on that joke?" he asked.

"Oh, there's no joke," she told him, sincerely, shaking her head. "I'm laughing because I'm happy. and I'm happy because I realize how much I love you." After a pause, she softly added, "I love you more than words can say."

His smile widened to a sexy grin that nearly stole away her breath. "Does this mean you'll marry me?"

Now it was her turn to toss him a flirty grin. "You'd better believe it."

He shouted in utter delight, rolling her back onto the bed, his mouth covering hers with an ardent kiss that promised a forever of happiness and joy.

* * * * *

In November,
be sure to look for Travis's story
THE DOCTOR'S MEDICINE WOMAN
as SINGLE DOCTOR DADS
continues…only fron Donna Clayton
and Silhouette Romance!

Silhouette invites you to come back to Whitehorn, Montana...

MONTANA MAVERICKS

WED IN WHITEHORN—
12 BRAND-NEW stories that capture living and loving beneath the Big Sky where legends live on and love lasts forever!

M·M

And the adventure continues...

October 2000—
Marilyn Pappano *Big Sky Lawman* (#5)

November 2000—
Pat Warren *The Baby Quest* (#6)

December 2000—
Karen Hughes *It Happened One Wedding Night* (#7)

January 2001—
Pamela Toth *The Birth Mother* (#8)

More MONTANA MAVERICKS coming soon!

Available at your favorite retail outlet.

Silhouette®

Where love comes alive™

Coming in November 2000
Based on the bestselling continuity series

An original
Silhouette Christmas Collection

36
HOURS:

THE CHRISTMAS
THAT CHANGED
EVERYTHING

With stories by

MARY LYNN BAXTER
MARILYN PAPPANO
CHRISTINE FLYNN

'TIS THE SEASON…
WHERE TIME IS OF THE ESSENCE
IN THE SEARCH FOR TRUE LOVE!

Available at your favorite retail outlet.

Where love comes alive™

Silhouette®

You're not going to believe this offer!

In October and November 2000, buy any two Harlequin or Silhouette books and save $10.00 off future purchases, or buy any three and save $20.00 off future purchases!

Just fill out this form and attach 2 proofs of purchase (cash register receipts) from October and November 2000 books and Harlequin will send you a coupon booklet worth a total savings of $10.00 off future purchases of Harlequin and Silhouette books in 2001. Send us 3 proofs of purchase and we will send you a coupon booklet worth a total savings of $20.00 off future purchases.

Saving money has never been this easy.

I accept your offer! Please send me a coupon booklet:

Name: _____

Address: _____ City: _____

State/Prov.: _____ Zip/Postal Code: _____

Optional Survey!

In a typical month, how many Harlequin or Silhouette books would you buy <u>new</u> at retail stores?

☐ Less than 1   ☐ 1   ☐ 2   ☐ 3 to 4   ☐ 5+

Which of the following statements best describes how you <u>buy</u> Harlequin or Silhouette books? Choose one answer only that <u>best</u> describes you.

☐ I am a regular buyer and reader

☐ I am a regular reader but buy only occasionally

☐ I only buy and read for specific times of the year, e.g. vacations

☐ I subscribe through Reader Service but also buy at retail stores

☐ I mainly borrow and buy only occasionally

☐ I am an occasional buyer and reader

Which of the following statements best describes how you <u>choose</u> the Harlequin and Silhouette series books you buy <u>new</u> at retail stores? By "series," we mean books within a particular line, such as *Harlequin PRESENTS* or *Silhouette SPECIAL EDITION.* Choose one answer only that <u>best</u> describes you.

☐ I only buy books from my favorite series

☐ I generally buy books from my favorite series but also buy books from other series on occasion

☐ I buy some books from my favorite series but also buy from many other series regularly

☐ I buy all types of books depending on my mood and what I find interesting and have no favorite series

---

Please send this form, along with your cash register receipts as proofs of purchase, to:
In the U.S.: Harlequin Books, P.O. Box 9057, Buffalo, NY 14269
In Canada: Harlequin Books, P.O. Box 622, Fort Erie, Ontario L2A 5X3

(Allow 4-6 weeks for delivery) Offer expires December 31, 2000.

PHQ4002

COMING NEXT MONTH

CMN1000